Margarita

The Case of The Numbers Kidnapper

Margarita

The Case of The Numbers Kidnapper

MICHELE WALLACE CAMPANELLI
National Best Selling Author

ARPress
45 Dan Road Suite 5
Canton MA 02021

Hotline: 1(888) 821-0229
Fax: 1(508) 545-7580

Ordering Information:
Quantity sales. Special discounts are available on quantity purchases by corporations, associations, and others. For details, contact the publisher at the address above.

Printed in the United States of America.

ISBN-13:   Softcover   979-8-89330-182-3
              Hardcover   979-8-89330-183-0
              eBook   979-8-89330-184-7

Library of Congress Control Number: 2024902547

Table of Contents

Chapter 1 1
Chapter 2 6
Chapter 3 10
Chapter 4 16
Chapter 5 20
Chapter 6 25
Chapter 7 30
Chapter 8 35
Chapter 9 38
Chapter 10 42
Chapter 11 46
Chapter 12 53
Chapter 13 58
Chapter 14 62
Chapter 15 67
Chapter 16 73
Chapter 17 79
Chapter 18 86
Chapter 19 94
Chapter 20 102
Chapter 21 106
Chapter 22 111
Chapter 23 115
Chapter 24 122

With deep appreciation for my family, I dedicate this book to:

Louis Campanelli's big heart,

Fontaine Wallace's brilliant mind,

David Wallace's brotherly support

And in loving memory of Margaret Athans.

A special thanks goes out to God, all the Wallaces & the Campanellis, my nieces Allyson & Kelsi, my nephew Chris, Marilyn Henderson, Steve Chandler, Dawn Kreiselman, Melisa Fearn, Ciera Parham, Nicole Jenkins, Jim & Loretta Pauline,Betty Duhamel, Courtney McClure, Robert Paniccia, Chris & Margie Long at Boggie Creek Airboat Rides, Johnny Butler at Lone Cabbage Fish Camp, Darold Hite or. at Camp Holly Fishing & Airboats, Writer's Digest school, Officer Steve Sigety, Kay Allenbaugh and Brandi Kroetch-Rafferty at Hollis books for believing In me and/or assisting with research for this project in the Title IX series.

Chapter 1

Definitely female. Her reflection in the mirror only reminded her of why Dante's friends downstairs were laughing; her raven hair was too long, her breasts were too obvious and her soft gray eyes could never look intimidating. Penny leaned away from the mirror, still feeling she knew more about the game of football than half the guys still bellowing about her below.

"I'm sorry, Penny." Louis apologized in the bedroom doorway. "I thought if I suggested you'd play, they wouldn't mind."

She turned on the television in the right corner of her room and flipped through the channels until she reached the Dolphin game. "That's okay." She knew it wasn't Louis' fault.

"Are you all right?"

To hide her Feelings, she picked up the newspaper, then crossed to her bed, glancing at the headline, "Basketball Player Missing."

"Are you?"

Still trying to veil her disappointment, she said. "Uh-huh. You'd better hurry before Frank or Dante let someone else play your position."

When he left, she dropped the paper and stepped Over to the large bay window that overlooked the giant back yard. The bright green grass spanned half the four-acre lot to the edge of the Indian River. After her twin brother Dante made the Bulldog team earlier this year, their father converted the back property into a football field with large plastic goal posts that sometimes fell down during the heavy Florida rain.

Boys gathered at the center, breaking up into two teams. She opened the blinds wider to watch them. They didn't know she did this every week. Each Sunday during football season, she turned away from the Sports Section or the game on TV and studied her brother's team's every move and attempted plays. She wanted to be out there so badly it hurt. Sometimes she saw herself among them, tossing the ball to Louis as no one had ever done before. She knew his breaks, even when he slowed down because he wasn't sure where the ball would drop. Louis seemed part of her out there on the field.

"Why do you kids insist on blaring the television and yelling while your Father is sleeping on the patio?" Her mother drifted into her room, snapping on a set of sparkling earrings.

"Not me -Dante's friends were making all the noise."

Her mother flipped back her dark permed hair and flared her pug nose. "Your father's on call this weekend. He needs all the shut eye he can get."

"I'll make sure, we keep quiet."

"Can you do me one more favor? I'm helping Mrs. Percy at the church bazaar this afternoon." She turned on a high heel to lower the television volume. "Take some drinks out to the boys in an hour. Tell them they must take a break. It's nearly 90 degrees today."

"Okay." Penny's heart pounded. She now had an excuse to go outside and be closer to the gridiron. "Bye, Mom."

After forty minutes, she couldn't stand the wait any longer. She rushed downstairs, filled glasses with water and hurried onto the screened patio.

Her father was snoring, with half his lanky body hanging over the bamboo futon. Seeing him like this made it hard to picture him as one of the state's best heart surgeons. Penny tiptoed past him and walked out into the yard.

"Come and get it!"

Louis dropped the ball and rushed toward her. "Hey." He slicked back his brown hair to keep the sweat from dripping into his hazel eyes. "How's the Dolphin game?'

Of all Dante's brawny, oversized friends, Penny found the smaller, thinner Louis the most friendly and handsome. He always made a point to talk with her about sports, schoolwork, music, any subject on his mind at the time. He didn't have the rich beachside manner or the perfect suntan; his nose looked kind of big for his round, scruffy face. Still, he was very sweet, cared about her opinions and every Sunday when he wore his see-through #17 jersey and the athletic shorts that clung to his tight bottom like glue, Penny found it hard not to admire his Physique.

"I don't know. I think the Jets are winning."

He took a glass and drank the water down in two giant gulps. "Figures."

Dante joined them, wrapping a towel around his neck and patting down his wet, rippled muscles. "So you want to be a quarterback, Sis"

"I can throw."

His face reddened as he held back his laughter. "Of course you can."

Louis grabbed the tray out of her hand and placed it in the grass as the others headed for the shady, date palm trees near the house. "Let's see what she's got."

"You're kidding, right?" Dante said.

"Nope You still want to try, Penny?"

She nodded, hardly believing she was being offered the chance. Her brother David had been the last one to ask. He was seventeen when he was killed in a crash by a drunk driver. She was only ten, proud and idolizing him for spending his days trying to teach her how to handle the football.

She loved when David would yell, "Penny's the greatest football player in sports today," when she ran as fast as she could and got under the ball in time. Once when she bobbled it in front of David's college recruiters, quick tears sprang to her eyes as a scout jeered. David ordered the man out of the yard and tossed his school's application in the trash. Seven Years. and she still missed him every single day of her life.

Louis said. "I'm going to go center and break right."

Penny nodded and lunged back into her stance the way David had taught her a decade ago. She cocked her arm, feeling the adrenaline rush, then threw the ball. Louis ran forward. He looked back, once, twice, then on his third attempt the ball was right next to him. He broke right and caught it in front of the goal post.

"Holy cow!" She had tossed the football over fifty yards. She jumped up and down and screamed with glee.

"You couldn't do that again if your life depended on it!" Dante yelled.

Louis ran to her, picked her up and twirled her around. "That was awesome! I knew you had it in you!"

"Put my Sister down!"

Louis did, grinning. "She's got an arm just like David!"

"Even if she's big enough to throw, it doesn't mean she's good in the pocket, or that she can take a hit!" Dante Said.

"We won't know what she can do unless we let her try." Louis returned the ball into her hands. "With a pass like that, when Gordan and Larry can't make it, she could be their replacement."

"Not in my lifetime!" Dante headed for the house.

"I'm not playing with any chick!" One of the boys yelled.

"Me either!" sneered another.

Before long only Louis and Penny remained in the backyard field. Guilt at stopping the practice filled her. "I'm sorry, Louie," she said, calling him by his nickname.

"About what?" He cocked his head, then gave her a bright smile. "We don't need them to teach you. I will."

"Really?"

"Why not? It's fun chasing a deep ball. I haven't done that in a while." He ran back out onto the field.

"Come on, show me that magic arm again!"

Chapter 2

"I'd like to speak to you both in my office." Dr. Margarita held the door open. Penny followed Louis inside her father's home studio. She immediately noticed that this formidable room had just been cleaned by Stella, their maid. She surveyed the large Square area of mahogany furniture. The bookshelves were in order. Medical files had been neatly placed in the cabinet and the maroon and black oriental rug had been cleaned. Her father's dirty footprints no longer Marked his entrance from playing golf yesterday with his best friend, Max.

Dr. Margarita Pointed to the two leather chairs near the desk. "Please, sit down," Penny suddenly had the strange sensation that she had done a bad thing.

"Is something wrong?"

"I saw you two outside " While Louis sat, Dr. Margarita made himself Comfortable by unfolding his lanky body into his reclining chair. He swayed slightly and his grey-white hairy feathered by the air conditioning draft. "Thanks to Dante's loud cussing waking me up."

Louis cleared his throat, obviously wrestling with his next choice of words. "Penny has a strong pass and I thought that it would be okay if I showed her a few things." He Squirmed a bit. "Am I in trouble for that?"

"No, no," Dr. Margarita showed a hint of a smile. "I think of you like another son. I appreciate your helping her when Dante didn't want you to."

Louis brightened. "He'll get over it."

"It's amazing coming from the background that you have, how good a man you're growing up to be." Dr. Margarita picked up the frame from his desk containing a picture of his late son. "I haven't seen that kind of character in a young man since David."

"Thank you, Sir."

"Not to mention, one with as much talent either."

Louis's cheeks flushed.

"You two really have something special. That kind of fellowship can't be duplicated. It wins games. It's called heart." Dr. Margarita put down the snapshot, staring at Louis with his dark blue eyes. "Do you think you could come a few hours earlier next Sunday before Dante's practice? I want to work with you to teach Penny a few more things."

"You do?" He raised a wary brow.

Penny gasped. "That would be awesome!"

"It's been quite awhile since I played, but I think I can handle instructing another of my kids to stay away from blitzing linebackers."

Louis agreed, "Sounds like a plan, but what linebackers is she ever going to play against."

"Honey," Dr. Margarita turned to her, "I want to ask you a question and I want you to be completely honest with me."

"Sure, Dad."

"Do you want to play football? I mean, really play like Dante and Louis do?" Penny's heart raced. She knew that's what she wanted more than anything. Her father's sudden question gave her the courage to finally say it out loud. "Yes."

"For the Indialantic High Bulldogs?"

"Yes!"

"Then you'll need lots of training before next year's tryouts. If Louis will help me, I think we can get you ready to impress Coach Barr."

"Are you serious, Dad?

"Serious as a heart attack. If I offer to pay Dante's friends twenty dollars an hour each Sunday morning they show up to help us train you, I'll get a few more players to come."

Louis bit his lower lip. "You want to employ the Bulldogs?"

"For now, I'll have to."

"I'll spread the word around." Louis cupped his hands on top of the desk. "At first they might laugh. For twenty bucks an hour, though, you may get half the team to come."

"Good, that's exactly what I want. Make sure you tell everyone, even third stringers. They'll get a chance to play in my back yard."

Louis checked his watch. "My Dad has an AA meeting, Sir. I have to make sure he attends."

"Then he's back on the wagon?"

"For now." Louis said. "He hasn't taken a drink in two weeks."

"That's wonderful. Take care." Dr. Margarita shook Louis' hand, firmly. "Thank you again for today."

"Before I leave," Louis Stood, "I want to say that Penny is very lucky to have a father like you. Someone who cares about her feelings." He opened the door. "Mine has never even come to one practice, let alone a game."

Speechless, Penny smiled up at him.

"If this is what you really want, Penny, I'll do everything in my power to make you great. It won't be easy, probably the hardest thing you've ever done. There are hand signals, plays, reading defenses, so much to memorize. Football isn't all glamorous, either there's pain and lots of it too."

"You can't talk me out of it," she announced. "I want to be a quarterback just like David, even better."

Louis said, "Dr. Margarita, I'd feel weird taking your money. I'm going to help Penny because I believe in her."

She turned to him, her stomach caught in her throat. Louis wasn't rich. He could have used the extra cash her father was handing out. "Thanks," she said, his faith in her tugging at her heartstrings. Indeed, their friendship was priceless.

That following Sunday, Louis showed up along with seven new, third stringer employees. This time, she didn't stay in her room reading the newspaper or watching the game from the window; she was a part of the action. It was incredible! She felt more alive than she ever had in her entire life.

Chapter 3

Ten months later...

The day of the team tryouts, Penny's excitement dimmed temporarily as she dialed Louis' number, praying he hadn't left yet.

"Hello?"

"I'm so glad you're still there!"

"Penny -what's up?" She let out a long breath. "Dante left me."

"He forgot you were going to tryouts?"

"I think he decided not to wait for me. I was, getting my stuff together when I heard his Firebird start. Next thing I knew, he drove off without me. The jerk!"

"No sweat. I'll be there in a few minutes."

"Thanks, Louie. I'll be waiting outside."

Relieved that she didn't have to wake either of her parents, Penny gathered her gear and hurried downstairs.

Her father was in his boxers, drinking a cup of coffee in the kitchen. "Dad, you're awake?"

"Couldn't sleep," Dr. margarita admitted. "I heard Dante tear out of here like a chicken with its head cut off."

"Yeah, great brother," she rolled her eyes.

"He'll be punished," her father decreed. "Let me throw on some pants. I'll drive you"

She felt guilty that he had gotten out of bed.

"Dad, you can go back to sleep. Louie's on his way."

Dr. Margarita yawned. "He'll take care of you then."

"Yes," Penny agreed, knowing that out of all her family and few friends, it was Louis she counted on the most. "He will."

"After you pass Driver's Ed in the fall, I'll get you your own car. This spring you won't have to depend on Dante or Louis to take you to school anymore."

"Thanks, Dad." Penny headed for the front door.

"Honey," her father called, putting down his cup of coffee. "Knock em' dead."

She smiled over her shoulder, "I will."

"Next time I see you, you'll be a Bulldog."

"I'm going to try my best." She could hear the rusty, old red pickup truck barreling down South Patrick Road. It wasn't a chariot made out of gold but it might as well have been. It was taking her to the kingdom of guts and glory that she's determined to conquer.

Penny rushed onto the driveway and swung the truck's door wide. "Hey."

Louis pushed down some fast-food garbage to make a place for her next to him. "Good morning."

She got in, noticing the two young men packed like sardines in the back seat. They were staring at her and she recognized them at once. "Hi, Frank, Jacob."

They were first stringers, some of the best players on the team. Frank was enormous. His neck is the size of the average woman's thigh. Intimidating and short-tempered, he lived up to the red-hair image. His mood swings often led him into trouble.

The fellow sitting to his right was Jacob. He was a real character, a class clown with fuzzy sandy hair and funky square glasses. In most schools he would have probably been considered a nerd, Penny thought, but he was a spectacular running back and for that he was popular.

Besides Louis, Penny appreciated Jacob's talent and his personality. He was a decent enough fellow. When Penny bumped into him around school or in town, Jacob always said hi instead of ignoring her.

"So you're really going to try out for our football team?" Jacob sounded intrigued. "I thought that was just a joke going around campus last year."

"Shut up," Louis snipped.

Jacob steeled himself. "I was just talking. I hear from Mike she's pretty good."

"Better than Gordan McLoy," Louis gave his opinion. "Wait until you see how she hands off the ball, right into your chest."

Frank pretended to cough, but under his breath Penny clearly heard, "No way."

"Want to walk to school, Frank?" Louis clenched his hands tighter onto the steering wheel.

Frank moved closer to Penny. His big head brushed in between her and the passenger's window. "Don't you ever want to put a dress? You might even be a hotty if you did. You're breasts aren't very big but your butt's as hard as a rock."

Louis's arm flew across Penny's chest and punched Frank square in the nose. Penny's eyes widened in horror as Frank plopped back into his crammed seat.

"He hit me!" Frank rubbed his face, showing Jacob. "Did you see that?"

Jacob said. "Your nose is bright red."

"Didn't hurt." Frank lied, "What'd you do that for?"

"For insulting a Lady!"

"Penny, a Lady?" Frank countered.

The road was dark and deserted this time of morning. Louis slowed down the truck and pulled off to the shoulder, "Get out, Frank!"

After a few moments passed with tension so thick a knife couldn't cut through it, Penny spoke up. "Frank, we don't want to be late our first day."

Frank mumbled, obviously worried about the time too. "Sorry."

Penny nodded in acceptance even he had been out of line.

"Penny your girlfriend, Louis?" Jacob wondered. "You're acting like she is." Louis didn't reply. Penny raised her gaze wondering why he didn't answer. Their eyes met, hazel to lavender, bonding together with a simple understanding of mutual attraction.

Frank asked, "Does Dante know you have a crush on his sister?"

Jacob gave his opinion. "Even if he does like her, Frank Louis is practically his best friend. Dante won't mind."

"Like hell he won't!" Frank commented as they approached Indialantic High's gym. "He'll hate the idea of anyone thinking of his sister as a piece!"

"You re really a jerk, Frank." Louis said.

"I wouldn't waste my breath talking to Dante about this." She had forgotten that Bulldog football players spread gossip faster than the cheerleaders.

"Dante doesn't care about anything that concerns me.

Louis disagreed. "Yes, he does."

"So what if he hates her?" Frank chuckled. "He's still going to flip out when he hears this!"

Louis gave him a warning. "Keep your mouth shut or you won't have any teeth when try to tell him!"

"Yeah, Frank. That's their business." Jacob continued. "Be nicer to her. What if she becomes our new quarterback?"

Penny's mouth curled up. Glad not everyone was so against her becoming a Bulldog.

"You need a ride home, Jacob?" Louis asked.

"Sure, if it isn't any trouble."

"What about you, Penny?" Louis inquired. You want to ride back with me or Dante?" }

"You," there was no doubt in her mind.

Louis parked the truck in front of the three story brick building with a large gray Bulldog head with snarling teeth painted on the side. Quickly, he jumped out, went around the truck and helped Penny down.

Frank followed her from that side, squeezing his overweight frame out of the back. "I need someone to take me home too, aren't you going to ask me?"

Louis gave Penny a wink as he grabbed her gym bag. "What do you think Penny? Should I?"

Penny fluttered her lashes. "Oh, I guess. He needs a little make-up for his freckles, but his butt is fine, I guess he's okay enough to ride with."

"Very funny." Frank retrieved his bag. "We'll see how you manage to survive tryouts. You're the one that won't be needing a ride anymore."

For the past three weeks, Penny had given it her all. Bruised, battered and sore all over, she kept her head held high as she walked beside Louis through the hallway to the bulletin board outside the gym. Her heart was pounding with anticipation. Just a few more feet; her answer posted on a single piece of white paper. Was she a Bulldog or wasn't she?

When they reached the hanging wooden board, the boys in front of the list opened up a space, their eyes gaping in absolute shock. Penny knew by their expressions and the few grins from the third stringers that she had made the team. She didn't even need to check for her name to know it was there.

Jacob, the one standing closest to Louis, suddenly patted her on the back, "Congratulations, Penny, maybe you'll even get to play if Gordan's knee acts up again."

Frank whirled Jacob around by his shirt and smacked him against the wall. "Don't you give that thing your blessing! All of us are going to Coach! We're not going to play with any girl, got it?"

Dante glared at Louis. "You're coming with us, right, to complain?"

Louis pointed to the paper. "No, Penny's name is two lines down from mine. I'm going to respect Coach Barr's decision. So should you, Dante."

Dozens of boys began to gather around Frank. Like soldiers going off to war in troop formation, they began marching towards the Head Coach's office.

Penny stayed behind with Louis supportively behind her. Around them were the third stringers who worked for Dr. Margarita. They were with Louis and Penny who didn't stand alone anymore.

Louis lifted his arm and put it around her shoulders. "Don't mind Frank," he said. "Or any of the rest of them."

She tried not to break down.

"You deserve to play," someone else added.

Penny wiped her watering eyes. "I'm not upset. I just can't believe I did it!" She twirled into Louis's arms, happily, jumping up and down. "I'm a Bulldog!"

The others cheered, emphatically.

Chapter 4

Penny decided to celebrate by treating herself to her favorite vice, ice cream. After Louis dropped her off at home, she strolled down the block to the Eau Gallie Shopping Plaza to Deli's Freeze, the comer ice cream shop.

She had wanted Louis to join her, but didn't know how to ask him. Ever since Frank questioned if he has a crush on her, Louis hadn't offered to take her out anywhere other than to school and back. She wondered if Louis hadn't answered because he didn't want to hurt her feelings.

She entered the fifties-styled, black and white checkerboard parlor and Searched through the glass displays, making sure her favorite flavor in a ten gallon container was available. "The usual please."

The server flipped open the lid and began stuffing two scoops of rocky road into a large waffle cone. She handed Penny the dessert in exchange for two dollars. "Thank you for Coming to Deli's Freeze. Have a nice day."

Penny sat at a booth near the glass window, watching the people carrying bags of groceries and clothing from the shops in the strip. She licked the top and savored the smooth taste of cool, rich chocolate.

A flash of light caught her attention. Reflecting the bright sunshine, a dark blue sedan pulled in front of the store, scaring off the morning doves in its path. A moment later, a brawny man in his fifties emerged. Bearded and handsome, Penny recognized Max Parker, her father's best friend, who reminded her of James Bond. More because of what he did for a living than the way he looked or spoke. Over the past seven years in America, Max's British accent has nearly disappeared. He claimed he had to lose it being an undercover police officer for Indialantic. She guessed it worked. He was the best in Brevard at solving strange homicides and catching the robbers of Indialantic's oceanside homes.

Penny waved.

He motioned for her to come out. "It will only take a second," he mouthed.

Penny went outside then jumped on top of his vehicle's hood to sit. "Let me guess, Dante is in trouble again. What did he do this time, knock down another mailbox?" She nibbled off a marshmallow on the top of her cone.

"No," he answered.

"My Dad cheat at golf last weekend?"

Max took a deep breath and wiped his fingers through his salt and pepper hair. "I'm glad I found you. I need to talk to you, man to woman."

Penny swallowed the marshmallow. "What about?"

"Your being a football player."

She shook her head. "Oh no, not you, Uncle Max." She called him by his nickname. "You can't be against my becoming a Bulldog?"

"So you made the team?"

"Yes, why is that a problem?"

"There have been some disappearances of young female athletes recently in the southern states. Five all together are missing: a gymnast, a hockey player, a soccer goalie, a softball player and one of the Noles."

She remembered seeing a newspaper headline. "Alexandra Martin, I read about her in the "Alexandra Martin, I read about her in the newspaper. I didn't know anything about the others."

"They're from different states, Alabama, Georgia, South Carolina and now Florida. All the Departments assumed they were runaways. Then Alexandra Martin vanished from Florida State. She's got a 4.0 average and volunteered for a runaway hot line. One of her fellow teammates remembered Martin getting threatening E-mails so the FBI got involved." Max placed his hand on her arm comfortingly. "They're trying to connect the kidnappings. They suspect we may very well have another serial killer in the southern states."

"Who are the athletes missing?"

"Karen Dubin, Cindy Cambell, Janis Teller, Dawn Kresil and Alexandra Martin." Max tightened his grip. "Have you recently gotten anything suspicious in the mail or on the computer?"

"No," she felt a nut dripping down her hand and licked up. "But, Uncle Max, I'm not famous like those girls."

"You'd tell me wouldn't you?"

"Of course," she promised. "You'd be the first one I would."

"Good."

"So what order were the girls taken?" She said. "If you don't mind my asking."

He looked at her. "What do you mean?"

"Were they reported missing in the order you just told me."

"Karin Dubin vanished first, Cindy Cambel was second, then came Janis Teller, Dawn Kresil and Alexandra Martin."

Penny pictured the girls playing their sport in her mind's eye: Karen Dubin in her gymnast tights, Cindy Cambell in her hockey jersey, Janis Teller kicking a soccer ball, Dawn Kresil pitching underhanded for her softball team and Alexandra Martin jumping up to slam dunk a basketball. "Uncle Max, these girls are being taken by number."

He gasped. "What?"

"The number on their uniforms. Karin wears number 1, Cindy 11, add that together that's 2, Janis 3, Dawn 22 which is 4, Alexandra wears 41 that equals 5."

"How did you come up with that?"

"Easy. Things happen fast on a football field. I can't see the face of the person I'm supposed to be throwing to most of the time. I search for jersey numbers first."

"That could be a possibility. I'll contact the FBI right away and let them know your theory."

"Glad I could help!" She exclaimed.

"Jolly good. You very well could be a genius."

"No big deal."She jumped down from the unmarked police car, taking another bite.

"Thank you." Max relayed a warning. "Just please be careful, Penny. There aren't many female football players. I would hate for you to become another notch on that bugger's belt no matter what number you decide to start wearing."

"Don't worry. I'll call you if someone starts bothering me."

"If anything happened to you, I don't know if your Dad or I could take it. Losing David was enough for one lifetime."

As he drove away, Penny wondered why such a thoughtful man never got married or had children of his own. She was glad, though, that he hadn't. as her father's confidante, he cared about her like a daughter and she felt comforted by his protectiveness for her and Dante.

Finishing the last of her cone, she strolled to the corner of the plaza. As she made the turn onto South Patrick road, she saw Louis's truck leaving her driveway. "Louis!" She jogged over. "Why'd you come back?"

He passed a large box out to her with the name Penny written on the top. "I forgot my playbook at school when I went back to the gym, look what I found."

Taking the box, she opened it. Inside was a pale blue jersey with "P. Margarita" written across the shoulders. She held it up and read what was below, the number she had chosen, the one David used to wear. Proudly, she smiled as she ran her hand over the number 8.

Chapter 5

Two thirds of the team were leaning against the outside gym wall, ignoring the Coach's first order to start calisthenics. They were protesting silently, but their meaning rang loud and clear enough: "If Penny Margarita keeps playing, we won't."

Among them were Frank Loden, Jacob Miller, Gordan McLoy, all the Varsity seniors including her brother Dante. She had hoped that Dante would have changed his mind by now. Even if he didn't care about her, she knew at least he liked Louis. Her brother had everything, stunning looks, decent grades, dozens of girlfriends. Still, he wouldn't even lift a finger to help her or his longtime friend. Her heart ached, knowing how he lived and breathed football. He must really hate her being there.

Dante dropped his gym bag. Penny kept her eyes on him while she and the rest of the Bulldogs started lining up for wind sprints. He stuffed his tanned hands into his jeans and shifted positions. One black sneaker crossed the other. His solid jawline tightened and he bite his lower lip, gazing angrily back at her with his dark blue eyes.

"Those who aren't on this field in two minutes for warm-ups will be cut!" the Coach roared. "Do I make myself clear?"

"No girl is going to be my backup quarterback!" Gordan McLoy removed his Bulldog jacket from his tall frame. He raised it high above his sandy brown mop of hair and threw it to the ground. "Not now or ever!"

Penny felt his hatred. It chilled her to the bone.

"We'll be the laughing stock of every school in the district if we keep her on our team!" Frank angrily added.

"One minute left." The Coach announced, his attention glued to his stopwatch. "30-29-..."

Then a miracle happened. Dante and Jacob moved. They started walking casually toward the line. She heard Frank order them to stay. When they got to the end Gordan started calling them names. Dante's eyes went coldly to hers as if to say, "You're making me do this, lose most of my friends."

"4-3-2-1," Coach raised his hand to the resisters. "Get out! Get out of here! You're cut from the team!"

Penny couldn't believe it. "Coach, all of them?"

"Who's in command here, me or them?"

Dante reminded him. "If she stays we won't be able to play on Friday, Coach."

Louis argued. "That's not true—we've got about twenty guys here. We'll play iron man football if we have to, play both sides."

"That's the spirit, Louis!" The Coach agreed.

Penny gave a halfhearted smile. Louis would stand by her no matter what. "We can't win like that. With a few injuries we wouldn't even qualify."

"Sure we can," Louis explained. "Most of us can play several positions."

"But not well," Penny retaliated. "If I stay, the Bulldogs waste a whole season. We won't be able to win a few games let alone get to the State Championship."

"Maybe I was wrong about you," the Coach grabbed her arm. "If you're so willing not to believe in your fellow teammates, you don't have the character I'm looking for in a starter."

"Don't you see, I have no choice but to leave, for you, the school and the good of the Bulldogs!" Penny ripped herself from the Coach's grasp and rushed away towards the girls' locker room. She couldn't stop herself. Like the wind, she raced, slamming the locker room door shut after she entered. She fell to the floor, mourning over her dying dream of playing football.

She stayed for hours, grieving, glad the soccer team didn't have practice today so she had a private space. When she finally got her tears under control, it was nearly four o'clock. She had no choice but to walk the one mile home since she had missed her ride with Louis.

She didn't get more than a block away when Louis pulled up in his father's beat up red truck.

"Get in." He drove off the road in front of her. "Dante and I have been looking all over for you. He's still at the school searching the halls."

"Go away."

He stopped the engine and jumped out. "Why are you letting us down? Gordan and Lester got cut. You're our only quarterback now."

"Not any more I'm not."

"You're right. Because real players never give up. They live for the game! That's all that matters, not the fact that those jerks didn't want you to play cause you're a girl. You just have to be out there even if it's on the bench." Louis matched her hurried pace. "If you're part of a team you don't jump ship during tough times. That's what separates the men from the boys. You stick by your team come hell or high water. You follow the Coach's orders because you love being part of the bigger picture."

"Maybe I love the Bulldogs enough; I'm willing to sacrifice my hopes and dreams so that they will have another season."

"Don't you believe in your abilities? he questioned. "We can't pull it off without Frank on defense or Gordan as our quarterback. He's had years to develop."

"We are magic, you and me. You're way better than Gordan. You know it. I know it. Even the Coach does. There's no telling how tight we can get or how far we can go! We could even get scholarships to a good college!"

"You want to play college ball?

"Of course I do, so I can go on to Arena football or even the NFL. There's no way I could afford to attend a good school without a scholarship."

Penny recalled how tragic his parents' divorce was and how upset Louis had been when his mother abandoned him for a new man in San Francisco. His father was an on-again, off-again drunk. Neither of them supported him. And out of all those guys that her father paid to practice with her, Louis had been the only one who hadn't taken a paycheck. He appreciated her talents enough not to take the money he could have used for college. She kicked a stone and felt even more dejected.

"Please, come back." Louis said softly.

She pivoted, changing directions towards the passenger side of the truck. To her surprise, Louis opened the door for her. She lifted herself onto a dirty seat covered with holes from where his dog Mitzy must have chewed. "What if the Coach won't let me return?"

"He will." Louis reached out and held her hand. "He said he would." She felt the heat rising from his fingers. Her blood began racing through her veins. He's everything she's ever wanted in a boyfriend, gorgeous, smart, kind, considerate, and so supportive. He's right beside her, touching her.

"It's up to you. What do you want?"

"You really think we can pull this off?"

"I know we can."

"How can you be so sure?" She tightened her grasp.

"Because I care about you and I know together we can do anything."

She couldn't keep herself from moving towards him. She was being pulled by invisible strings attached to her heart. She reached for him. His full masculine physique closed in on hers. Their lips met. Passionately, their kiss was stirring emotions inside her that she hadn't known existed; a giant wonderful paradise. How long had she wanted him to kiss her! Fire, stars and heaven mixed into one. Penny shook underneath the power of his kiss, enveloped in their tender embrace.

Dante's Firebird skidded to a stop in front of the truck. "What the hell is going on?"

Louis vaulted away from her. "I was just taking her home."

Dante ran over and grabbed Louis by the throat. "I can see that, straight to her bedroom." He shoved him against the truck.

Penny screamed. "Stop it!"

Suddenly laughter came from Dante, bellowing out. He dropped his hand to his stomach, bending over.

Penny knew at once. "He's joking with us."

"You really thought I was going to hurt you, Louie?" Dante slapped him on the back. "Kiss my ugly sister all you want. You're the crazy one who believes in her."

Chapter 6

Alone in the girl's locker room, Penny sat on the bench, staring in disbelief at the red painted words on the wall above her dressing area. "SHE IS WOMAN PHENOMENALLY! PHENOMENAL WITCH, DEAD IS SHE."

Who could have done this; Frank, Gordan?

Practice had gone well the past few weeks. The team had really come together to prepare themselves for tonight's home game against the Rockledge Raiders. Everyone seemed to accept her now, at least she thought so. Could it be just another cruel joke by her brother?

The girl's locker room door swung wide open. An eerie feeling washed over her in waves. "Is someone there?" All the cheerleaders were out the field. She could hear their chants, "We're ready! We' re back! Let's hear it for the Dogs, for the gray, blue and black!" No one was supposed to be here.

She heard footsteps coming closer. Penny shoved her blue jersey quickly over her head and shoulder pads. Thoughts of Uncle Max's missing athletes overwhelmed her. She grabbed her blue and gray helmet with the black paw print on the side, ready to swing. "Who's there?"

A girl stepped around the corner in plain view. Penny recognized Sarah McLoy who had played for the Bulldog volleyball team last year before moving on to FIT college.

"My name's Sarah. I'm Gordan and Kerry McLoy's sister."

Penny didn't know Kerry, but she knew Gordan too well. She wondered if his sister had written those words or if Gordan sent her here to beat her up before the game. She looked harmless enough with her short blonde hair, bright green eyes, and her pretty pink sundress, but Sarah McLoy was tough. Penny recalled Sarah hitting a boy in the lunchroom who spilled Jell-O on her sweater. Two teachers had to break up the fight, and the boy had to go to the infirmary.

"What do you want?"

Sarah studied her for a moment. "To wish you good luck tonight."

"Aren't you mad at me for Gordan being cut from the team?"

"lve had to live with his sexist attitude all my life. 1 enjoy watching him suffer because of it."

Penny understood. "I see."

Sarah stared at the red sentence. "Funny, that's the same color as Frank's new painted motorcycle."

Penny closed her locker and went to Sarah's side, suddenly feeling more at ease than she had all day. She felt right in her skin and in the #8 jersey with Margarita printed on the back.

Penny Margarita moved into the huddle with tne crowd cheering and the reporters from the *Florida Today* newspaper snapping pictures. She glanced toward the grandstands. Her Parents were waving at her with worried expressions written across their faces. Rockledge had the largest, best rated defense in the south and the Bulldogs were about to face them.

Her lavender eyes flashed to Louis. He gave her a big thumbs up, giving her the confidence to take a deep breath.

It had come down to this. Could she prove herself?

From the sidelines, the coach signaled a passing play into the right corner of the twenty-yard line. He must be depending on the other team not expecting her to be able to toss the ball down field. They clapped out of the huddle and went to maintain their positions.

"29,28, hut, hut," Penny lunged back. Louis was open down the sidelines. Her right hand spiraled out the ball with determination. Like an accurate gun, the speeding burct went for its target.

Whoosh! A Rockledge linebacker leaped and knocked it into the hands of a Defensive End. No one could catch that Raider. He ran untouched into the end zone.

"Interception! Touchdown Raiders!" yelled the announcer.

The people booed. Her first time out, first play, placed numbers on the board for the other team.

The next two quarters for the bulldog's offense went by just as badly, only 4 completions and no numbers placed on the board. The defense had to struggle every down to keep the Raiders from scoring again. In the third quarter the Raiders got all the way down to the two-yard line. Luckily, they managed to hold them to a field goal. Beginning of the fourth quarter: Bulldogs 0 Raiders 7.

Raiders punted weaky to the Bulldogs thirty-yard line. Special Teamster Tyrom Jackson, last year's third stringer, ran the ball to middle field.

Penny took front and center. They were going to surprise the Raiders by running the ball instead of sticking with the pass. She fell back into a stance, pay faked, then handed off to Jacob for a draw play.

The slow drive gained an average of six yards. "Never forget, football is 30% brawn 40% brains and 30% outsmarting the clock." David's words came haunting back to her. She started worrying that they were taking too much time to be able to score twice.

When they reached the twenty-yard line of Raider territory, Penny threw a quick screen pass to Louis. He outran his defender.

"Touchdown!" The announcer shouted over the loud speaker.

Bares 6 Raiders 10.

The Bulldogs went for two and succeeded with a running play that had the Rockledge defense chasing Jacob to the right corner of the end zone.

Five minutes left on the clock.

The Raiders made their way to the ten yard line. The defense stuffed them, keeping the Raider's offense to the short field goal.

Bulldogs 8 Raiders 13.

One minute until the buzzer.

The kick was good and trapped the Bulldogs on the Rockledge fifteen. Penny had waited for this moment all her life. If this game was to be won, it would be done by a quarterback's accurate arm. First play Penny threw at thirty-five yard pass which Louis caught in the middle of the Bulldog paw-print emblem center field.

She called time.

Forty seconds on the board.

Next play she got sacked by a Raider middle linebacker before she could get the ball off. Her gray and black helmet struck the ground so hard her hands went numb and she didn't know if that brilliant white light shining down on her was from the field lights or a pathway to heaven.

The Bulldog fans jumped to their feet, Screaming, "No!"

"Is she all right?" questioned the commentator. "This doesn't look good, Folks."

Penny shook her head and rose. She didn't even hear the crowd clapping; her mind was set on accompishing only one thing.

Second attempt, Jacob caught the ball but couldn't get out of bounds. Quickly they hurried for another play but Penny was forced to spike the ball to hold the clock down to four seconds.

This was it. Penny tried to remain calm as she tapped her helmet which symbolized Louis' most dreaded play, the Hail Mary. Penny knew he hated the Hail Mary, not knowing how far the wind would carry the ball.

She yelled over the crowd noise, "Go to the left corner of the end zone, don't look back until you get there and whatever you do, don't slow down!"

"Don't worry. The gas is on and the motor's running on overdrive."

With the snap, Penny dropped back and waited. She watched Louis run, measuring his speed and distance by how often his cleats tossed up the grass. The overweight defenders couldn't catch up. Louis was using all his strength to cover the ground into the end zone. She released the football straight up into the air. Louis turned around. The second he did, he lifted his hands and the ball fell right into his fingers.

Bulldogs 14 Raiders 13.

"Touchdown! Touchdown! The Bulldogs have won with a fifty yard touchdown!"

The crowd was on their feet. Penny rushed to Louis. When they met, they jumped into an embrace, slapping each other on the ass.

Teammates ran to them, hitting their helmets, cheering them on. And the Indialantic crowd stormed the field in one, unruly, celebrating mass of fans.

"Good game," Rockledge's Coach said to her.

She followed her players into the gym. The were waiting for the Coach to give a victory speech before they split up to shower.

We did it!" The Coach praised. "We beat the unstoppable Raiders and proved the critics wrong! We won because we worked as a unit! Next week, were pong to bite the hell out of the Hags! We've got a lot of work to do, but God help them. We've got a football team here in Indialantic!"

Chapter 7

Penny shifted her body on the ocean sand, feeling the waves roll in around Louis and her. They were Tying on the beach in their bathing suits. The sun was setting; the sky blazed a brilliant, purplish red.

She had never been so happy in all her life. The Bulldogs were undefeated, going to the regional game next Friday. Louis, the sweetest man on earth, leaned over to kiss her.

His lips tasted like chocolate. The ice cream from Deli's freeze still flavored his mouth. She relished the sweetness. Louis, mixed with her favorite treat, tantalized her senses.

Her hands feathered across his bare, tan chest, quivering over his muscles. Louis took her breath away. His every masculine curve causing her to want this moment to last forever.

A wave crashed Upon them. Penny hardly noticed the invasion of water except for her mouth stinging from the salt and her eyes seeing the glistening drops falling from his curly brown hair.

"Thank you for asking me out, Louis. How did you know I love Deli's?"

"Your father." He said above the roar of the ocean. "I told him I needed to spend time alone with you to talk."

She hoped he wanted to inquire if she'd be his girlfriend. "About what?"

"Someone wrote a note in my math workbook yesterday. I don't know how they knew what page the teacher would assign, but they did. Do you know anyone who would want to hurt you?"

"Why? What'd it say?"

He shook his head and sat up next to her. His big toes digging into the small sea shells. "Nothing worth repeating.

"Tell me." She raised herself onto an elbow.

Just at that moment, Dante yelled to them from the 5th Avenue boardwalk. He then jumped down the wooden steps on the dunes, jogging towards them. A brunette wearing a string bikini followed closely behind. "I didn't know you guys were coming to the beach today." Dante commented. "I would have come with you. This is Karen."

Penny acknowledged her but knew it would be some other cheerleader next week. "Hi."

"Are we still fishing on Sunday?" Louis asked him.

"Sure. You want to come with us, Sis?"

She raised an eye brow. "You want me to go on a fishing trip with the both of you? I thought you always said taking out the boat was a guy thing."

"I don't know. I just want you around that's all."

Dante being nice? Penny suspected immediately that he was up to something. She stood. "Okay, spill it."

He shrugged her off.

"Are you sick, Dante?" |

"No."

"Is Mom or Dad on their death bed?"

"I hope not."

"Louis said he got a strange note. Did you get anything like that? Are you worried about my safety too?"

Dante didn't deny it. "Somebody sprayed a message in shaving cream all around my car this afternoon after school."

"What did it say?"

"She is woman, hear her roar while she's falling to death's door."

"I'm going to talk to Uncle Max about this." She grabbed her beach towel.

"It's probably just Frank or Gordan." Louis said. "If it'll make you feel better, though, I'll go with you to talk to the cops."

"Don't you think you've done enough." Dante blocked their path. "You've already destroyed Frank or Gordan's chances of getting a good scholarship. Now you want to throw one or both of them in jail too!"

Penny kicked the sand. A small, brown crab flew several feet, landing next to a seagull. The big, white bird squawked then flew away from the shoreline. "Whoever's doing this should be in jail! Why do you always take their side? I'm your sister!"

Dante threw his hands up in the air. "Now you're scaring the wildlife!"

"I know you still like Frank and Gordan, but what they're doing is upsetting all of us. Got it?"

Dante checked out the crab. Its little claws were digging a new home for it to hide in. "That's the whole reason I didn't want you on the team in the first place. I knew this would happen. Not everyone's like me or Louis, we know when to shut up about equality. You're going to get hurt. And maybe I won't be around to help you."

Penny wrapped the beach towel around her and walked past him. "Is that a threat or a promise?" She didn't wait to hear Dante's response. She wanted to call Uncle Max from one of the pay phones on the boardwalk. There might be more to this than even Dante knew about.

She got as far as the steps and across the street before she noticed the dark sedan already parked at Shady Palm Surf Shop. "Uncle Max!" She called to her father's best friend.

He got out, not smiling. "I want you to meet someone." He pointed to the passenger in the car.

She peered in and saw a blonde haired man wearing a white buttoned down shirt and a striped gray tie. "Who is it?

"Agent Jack Sigety, FBI."

"FBI?" Penny gasped.

"They called the Indialantic PD. With all the press you've been getting, they're afraid the kidnapper may put you on his list."

The stranger stepped out of the car. He looked twenty-five or -six, but his giant brown eyes could easily make him appear younger than he is. He was thin with a solid build, and not very tall. She towered over him.

"Call me Jack." He held out his hand. "I'm quite a fan of yours, been reading all about your golden right arm."

"Thanks." She shook his hand. "Nice to meet you."

"Id like you to come down to our office near Patrick Air Force base. Do you know where that is?"

"Sure, near the Kennedy Space Center."

"Great, can you make it tomorrow?"

She thought about missing school or practice. "Sorry, we've got a big game on Friday. If we win, the Bulldogs get to go to the State Championships. Can I come next week?" |

"Next week it is then. A word of warning though, Miss Margarita, another young athlete is missing. Wendy Hamilton, have you ever heard of her?

"No."

She's a racecar driver, Her car's #6, sponsored by Alabama Motor sports."

Penny pulled the towel tighter. The ocean breeze chilled her as the sun faded din the sky. "The guy's up to number 7 then."

"The kidnapper is choosing his victims not only by number but also for outstanding ability in sports usually dominated by men. Since you are becoming popular and possess proven athletic skills, we've decided to keep you under surveillance. So if you should encounter anything out of the ordinary we want you to press this." He handed her a small black box with a red button in the center. "It sends an emergency signal directly to us."

"It's also a tracking device." Max informed. "In case you... well, that won't happen."

"I can't carry it during the game."

Jack Sigety pressed. "Don't worry, we'll be watching you twenty-four hours a day for the next few weeks and we'll have extra agents on duty for the Regional and Championship games. Have you received any threats?"

"Kind of, three."

"Why didn't you tell me?" Max raised his tone.

"I thought someone at Indialantic High was mad about being cut from the Bulldogs. Whoever did it knows which gym locker I use and what math class my boyfriend takes, even what car my brother drives." Penny saw Louis coming up the boardwalk steps behind two surfers carrying boards. "I didn't think the pranks were related."

"They might be," Max said.

"Can we talk about this later? I don't want Louis to know about all of this."

Louis jogged over, putting his arm around Penny. "Here you are." He smiled at Max Parker. "Hi, Uncle Max."

The officer scratched his gray beard. "Good to see you, Chap."

Chapter 8

The Bulldogs won by an explosive upset, 31 to 30, over the Canaveral Calvary. For the first time in Indialantic High history, the Bulldogs were ranked number one and would be going to the State Championship game in Tampa Stadium.

Bombarded by reporters, Penny found a clearing amongst the cameras and made her way toward the locker room to change before the press conference. The girls' changing room at Canaveral High was on the opposite side of the field from the boys'. Canaveral didn't offer many opportunities for woman's sports, not even a softball team. The locker room was next to the dance studio, beyond the gym and down an isolated hallway.

She hardly felt the pressure through her padding when someone touched her shoulder. She turned. Max Parker smiled and said, "Congratulations."

"Thanks, Uncle Max."

"The locker's clear. There's a man posted outside. Here's the beeper." He handed her the black box.

Penny took it, reluctantly. She didn't want to think about her life being in any danger. Her greatest accomplishment shouldn't be darkened by fear. Not now, not after four fantastic quarters. Three touchdowns and no interceptions, what a night! Louis was right when he said they were magic. He caught balls that were way off. When she flopped, he prevailed. They were a great team. All the Bulldogs pulled together. The defense was incredible. Dante got four sacks and knocked Jim Lauderbon out in the first half.

What a game!

She pivoted around the corner, practically floating down the hallway. She heard footsteps and peered over her shoulder. Just Jack Sigety, keeping an eye on her. Another man stood ahead of her, wearing a dark suit.

"Good game," he said, opening the door to the locker room for her.

"Thanks, it was." Penny shut the door behind her. The lights were flickering but no one else was inside.

She moved to the bench where she had draped her clothes without bothering with a locker. With her own personal guard outside the door protecting them, she didn't have any reason to.

It felt good to sit. She had a few bruises, but they got no sacks on her, not tonight. Her body was still in one piece, no serious injuries. She took a deep breath, relaxing. She appreciated having some time by herself to relish the moment.

She put down the FBI black box and began unlacing her cleats.

Just one more game this season. She could hardly believe she'd be going to the State Championship. It seemed like only days since her father and Louis started training her. Now, she'd become a high school football star like David.

If only he could have been here today to see her win. He would have loved every minute of it. He would have been there if he hadn't been for some drunk driver taking his life. He'd been gone seven years now and each year it got harder to deal with, Penny realized, especially now that she needs his advice. David would have been the perfect person to consult on the upcoming Championship game and the most critical decision of her life — which college to sign with. She'd already received twelve letters, the same number Louis had gotten and four less than Dante. All three of them were sent letters of intention from Western Florida University to play for the Bobcats with full football scholarships. That seemed like the best place if they wanted to stay together, but there were so many options. One university had promised she could become a starter her freshmen year.

She took off her jersey. The blue shirt was covered with dirt stains and sweat, her sweat. Only One more game to wear Margarita #8. She hoped wherever she went to college, they'd let her keep David's number.

She stood and began taking off the rest of her uniform and protective padding. She had to get ready for the press conference. The faster the question and answer session went, the earlier she would be on the bus sitting next to Louis, talking over the game with her friend and her teammates.

A banging noise came from the door's direction. She turned around but didn't see anybody entering.

"Witch!"

She looked right and left, no one. Was someone inside the locker room? Were they calling her that name? Footsteps were coming behind her, a hard heeled shoe hitting the tile mixed with an unusual dragging sound.

Realizing she wasn't alone, her left hand shot down toward the FBI beeper on the bench. It was only a foot away; with one swoop of a finger, the agent outside would rush in and she would be safe.

Wham! A baseball bat slammed into her left shoulder, stopping her from grabbing the box. She saw the long silver weapon being raised again toward her head. She lifted a defensive hurt arm, but too late. She felt the sharp impact, then her body falling. White stars flashed in her vision, followed by complete darkness as she lay still on the floor.

Chapter 9

Penny woke in a bright, white room. Her head throbbed. Tubes were poking out of her wrists and pain tingled down her left arm. Before her eyes could focus, Agent Jack Sigety leaned over her. "She's regaining consciousness."

Her father pushed him back. "You're in the hospital, Honey. You're doing fine. We're all here, your mother, Dante, and Louis. So rest, it will help you gain back your strength."

Penny glanced at her arm. A black and blue mark ran from her shoulder to her elbow. She had never felt so weak. She had no desire to speak to anyone, to eat or to return to sleep. She turned toward the window, trying to avoid closing her eyes, so she wouldn't see that descending bat again.

A male nurse entered the room. "Several of the Bulldogs downstairs want to talk to Penny. I told them she isn't allowed any more visitors at this time but they insisted she get these flowers."

Dr. Margarita tock the dozens of red, white and yellow roses. Their fragrance filling the room. "This one's from Tyrom." He read a card, then pulled out another. "Kevin, Jacob... there's a rose and a card from every member of the team it looks like."

Mrs. Margarita said, "Maybe one of them did this to her."

Jack Sigety took away the enclosure cards, "The FBI will need to examine these for fingerprints."

"Has anyone seen the morning paper?" Dante held up the news aper from the sofa. The headline read BULLDOG QUARTERBACK ASSAULTED!

Louis plopped down in the empty space beside Dante after leaving the bathroom. His eyes were swollen. His nose was red as if he'd been crying. Dante folded the paper away, then gave Louis his cup of coffee.

"She'll be fine, Louis," Dr. Margarita explained. "Her arm's bruised not broken and there's no fluid on the brain. The second MRI will concur that she can come home with us in the next day or so."

Penny, seeing Louis' sad expression, rolled her head in his direction and smiled.

"You awake?" He returned the smile.

She nodded.

Jack Sigety questioned. "So, Louis, did any of your teammates mention seeing someone fleeing the scene last night?"

"No," he replied.

"How about you, Dante? Remember more of what happened?"

"I already told you everything."

"Let's go over what you saw again." Jack Sigety pulled out a notepad from his jacket. "Maybe you'll recall something else."

"Do I have to?"

"Please, humor me."

Dante huffed, "I went to talk to my sister. I thought she played a great game and I wanted to tell her."

"You normally just walk in on your sister while she's getting dressed?"

"No, of course not, I knocked. When I didn't hear any response, I got worried and opened the door. I saw her lying on the floor next to a baseball bat. I yelled to the FBI guy to help and ran over to her. Then I heard a bang and looked up just in time to see a shoe disappear into the air conditioning duct. I tried to follow whoever it was but my shoulders were too big to fit in the vent."

"Describe the shoe."

Dante tapped his fingers on the table. "Hard heeled, like boot I think. It all happened so fast, I could be wrong."

"There were no prints on the bat except for Debra Jamison's. Are you sure you didn't see the assailant wearing gloves, or any other part of his clothing?"

"Like I said, just the shoe. The vent was pitch black inside."

"Why do you keep interrogating us when you're the ones who failed to protect her!"

Jack Sigety took responsibility. "You're right, the FBI should have held tighter security and had another agent posted inside."

"Why didn't you?"

"We felt the proper person wasn't available to make Penny feel comfortable."

"You mean a woman." Louis guessed.

"We weren't aware at that time of Debra Jamison's kidnapping either. We didn't learn about her until after we followed Penny to the hospital last night."

"Who is Debra Jamison? Is she a famous athlete? I've never heard of her." Dante commented.

"She plays for the Brevard County Little League. She's the only female on an all boy team, very talented for her age according to her father. The kidnapper choosing someone so young as number seven didn't fit his M.O."

"Is she going to be okay? Louis questioned.

"She's in ICU on the fourth floor. With the injuries she sustained during her escape, she's lucky to be alive. She jumped out of a moving vehicle. If the driver behind the van hadn't stopped and called for an ambulance, she might not have survived."

"You know what kind of car this guy drives?" Dante inquired.

"Yes, a white minivan with a handicap sticker in the window."

Penny turned onto her side. She tried to block out the conversation in the room but every word bounced right back at her. She had been attacked. Another girl's life is hanging in the balance. Penny was glad she wasn't permanently injured, but couldn't help thinking about the reality of the situation. Her enemy was still out there waiting for another chance at #8.

Chapter 10

The smell of smoke woke Penny in the middle of the night. Her head spinning, she scrambled for the button on the side of the bed to ring the nurses' desk and ask where it was coming from.

"Don't bother calling for help." Frank's face reflected in the window as a small match's flame lit the cigarette dangling in his mouth.

"Frank?"

"And Gordan." A big hand came forward and raised a quart container of ice cream with the word Deli on the side. "Dante mentioned that you have a fetish for rocky road."

Penny sat up, trying to stop herself from shaking. "How'd you two get in here?"

"We showed the FBI agent outside a picture from Dante's birthday party last year. It's of Louis and the three of us." Frank flashed the pictus of them with their arms around each other, then grabbed the hospital blanket at the foot of the bed and covered her to her waist. "We told him we were close."

She hadn't even realized that she had just been lying in front of them in a thin, white nightgown. "Please, leave."

"Everything okay in here?" The man who had been standing outside now peeked in. "Don't blow our cover." Frank whispered to her. "We just wanted to say we're sorry about this happening to you. We'd also like to apologize for treating you so bad at the beginning of the season."

"She doesn't care anymore, Frank. Let's get out of here before we get into trouble."

"I'm fine!" Penny yelled to the FBI Agent.

He shut the door.

"You two came to say you're sorry to me?" Penny repeated, unbelieving.

"Ever since I saw you play in that game against the Raiders, I realized that you really were a good quarterback." Frank put the chocolate carton and a plastic spoon down next to the bed on the night stand. "I should have given you a chance."

Gordan added. "We both should have."

"Now you think that I can play?"

"That's right." Frank switched on the light above her bed.

Penny's eyes blinked rapidly, adjusting. The two of them were at the side of her bed. Frank was pouring himself a glass of water while Gordan straightened up the newspaper Dante had left.

"We didn't write those words above your locker either. That wasn't us. Your cop friend Max questioned us about it. We wouldn't have done that." Frank added. "You're a royal pain, but you're still Dante's sister."

"Gee, thanks,"

"So when are you busting out of this joint?' Frank removed the cigarette from his lips and gulped down the water.

"I might be able to go home tomorrow if everything checks out today."

Frank put down the cup. "What you really need is to get that rock hard butt of yours back to win Indialantic High their first State Championship."

Penny lowered her eyes. "I can't."

"What?" Gordan grimaced. "You mean we treated you to rocky road just to find out you don't have gut's to finish out the year."

"Are you too hurt?" Frank asked.

"No."

"Then have you gone insane?" Gordan inquired. "This is for the Championship! What do you mean you can't?"

"You wouldn't understand."

"I do." Frank agreed. "You've got the skills. We bucked up and admitted that. We even felt sorry for you, being hit with a bat and all. No one deserves that, not when you can't help being a girl. The way I figure it, you're like a guy trapped in a female body."

Penny fought back her tears. "Just go."

Gordan stated. "You worked hard to get where you are. You've got the team believing in you, the whole school. You can't give up."

"I also have a maniac trying to kidnap me because of the number I wear."

"So change your number." Frank said matter-of-factly. "You're still better off than that girl in ICU!"

"You know about her?"

"Max told us a few things." Frank informed. "We just took a look at the kid. She's one living vegetable."

"Heartless," Penny closed her eyes. "You guys haven't changed a bit."

"No, you're wrong. Our whole lives changed because of you. Now you're trying to make it for nothing."

"I could be killed!"

"So, we all die. That's not the point you faced your fears just fine before now. I could have knocked you so hard in tryouts you wouldn't have been able to play at all. In fact, I tried. Hell, you kept getting right back up. You didn't give up your dream for me. How long have you known me since elementary school?" Frank reminded. "Why change your plans now because of some wacky stranger?"

"I should have never tried to play in the first place."

Frank grabbed Gordan by the jacks "Let's go. She's as done as that girl down in ICU."

"Yeah, a real loser." Gordan held up his hand in protest and left.

She heard them cuss all the way down the hall to the elevator. She felt terrible. They had come to apologize, but she had turned them away angrily and without acceptance.

Trying to rush after them, her foot got caught in the sheets and she stumbled out of bed. She quickly extended her hands and stopped herself from falling by grasping onto the window ledge.

With a deep breath of relief, she steadied herself.

Her hands clutched onto the sill, feeling something squishy underneath her fingers. She checked. A single duckweed, two tiny round leaves with thin string roots dangled beneath her fingers.

She hadn't seen a plant like this since she went boating in the shallow channels of the East Bay River. Locally, duckweed was found in either pond water or at Cypress Swamp. The small weed floats in groups over water. It colors the entire Cypress Swamp a bright shade of green, giving the snakes and alligators the opportunity to hide just below the surface.

Frank, Gordan, Dante or Louis must have gone fishing recently and got the weed stuck on some clothing, she thought.

She picked up the duckweed and dropped it into the wastebasket below. Several minutes passed. Two figures hurried into the night toward the parking garage. She yelled for Frank and Gordan to come back. They might not have heard her through the window. Either way, they didn't acknowledge her call. A few seconds later, a minivan peeled out of the large, cement structure, Penny trembled. Her knees gave way and she fell onto the hard floor. Gordan McLoy's minivan shone white in the parking lot lights.

Chapter 11

After Louis helped Penny from the hospital wheelchair into his truck, he stuffed in the accumulated bouquets of flowers and balloons.

"Uncle Max thinks I've gone off the deep end. I called him about Gordan having a white minivan. He told me there's an estimated one thousand white minivans in Brevard County."

Louis checked to make sure all the helium inflated "Get Wells" were still corralled before he shut the door. He hurried to the driver's side and got behind the wheel. "A lot of people drive minivans, Penny." He started the engine. With the sun beating through the windshield, she realized how crazy she must have sounded. Even In December temperatures peek in the eighties. White deflects the sun's heat and is Florida's most popular car color.

"Dante said your attacker must have been pretty small to fit into the air conditioning duct, remember? Frank and Gordan are huge.

"Yes," Penny watched the houses pass. In the driveways of several were minivans. In the three blocks they had driven from Regional Hospital, two had been white. "Uncle Max is right. I'm losing it."

"You're not. You've been through a lot these past few weeks." He placed his hand on top of hers, lovingly. "You're not going through this alone.

She smiled. "What would I do without you?' '

The red truck barreled over the Eau Gallie bridge. Pelicans perched below on me wooden pillars sticking out of the Indian River. While she watched a few took off into the azure blue sky; she thought about how lucky they were, to be able to fly. Wouldn't it be wonderful if she could soar away from the numbers kidnapper forever.

"I've been reviewing the letters from colleges lately. What do you think about Western Florida University?"

Penny avoided the question. "If that's where you want to play, sign."

"Dante likes Florida State."

"The Noles." Penny saw a white minivan pulling in behind them as they crossed the bridge. "What about the Gators, Hurricanes or the Golden Knights?"

"I don't care that much where Dante goes or where I play for that matter." Louis tightened his grip on her hand. "Just as long as we can stay together."

Pleased he was thinking of them as a "we," she didn't want him to know of her insecurities about returning to the game. "That sounds nice." Her eyes kept looking back to the white minivan trailing behind them.

"So then WFU is a great choice?" He turned the truck at the corner and headed down South Patrick Road toward Penny's house in Doctor's Row, a local nickname. "You'd like being a quarterback for the Western Florida Bobcats?"

"I don't want to talk about colleges, right now?"

"You can't think of them because you're scared that the nut's still after you, right? Don't worry; the FBI will catch him. For now, you have the entire Indialantic Police force, the FBI, Dante and me."

Cars were parked in the yard of her house, dozens of them. Two had metallic signs on the side, "Martha Catering", another delivery truck read, "Wells Flowers." Penny asked Louis, "Are Mom and Dad throwing a party?"

"A welcome home one for you." Louis spilled the beans. "Everyone on the team is invited to celebrate your recovery and the Bulldogs going to the Championship. Even Frank and Gordan are coming tonight.

She grabbed the wheel, horror gripping her heart. "Let's get out of here!"

"Penny, your Dad spent the whole day decorating the house and inviting everybody."

She held her hands in front of her face. "Keep driving, Louis, or I'll never forgive you!"

Louis rolled the truck back onto the road. "What's gotten into you?"

"I don't want to see anyone, especially the team."

"Why not?"

"What if that monster is one of them?"

"He isn't a Bulldog. The guy who attacked you is small. Besides, Coach Barr could change your number to 1 or 2. That way you'll no longer be 8. He won't come after you again. Even if he does, the FBI is doubling the agents to protect you. They're following us right now, four cars down."

Penny glanced at the sideview mirror. She didn't see any FBI, just the minivan switching lanes to pass the truck. Catching her attention, Penny noticed it gaining speed, then who was sitting on the passenger's side, Sarah McLoy. Penny raised her head, wondering. "Is that Gordan?" Penny asked Louis.

Louis glanced up. "It's Sarah McLoy, their sister."

"No, who's driving?"

He craned his neck to see around Sarah just as the vehicle raced past. "Their Dad."

Louis's eyes turned to her, bulging. "You still think Frank or Gordan are guilty, don't you?"

Penny shook her head. "I don't know."

"The air conditioning vent in the girl's locker room is not that big, Penny. How could a football player fit through it?"

"How small is it?"

Louis stomped the gas pedal and turned down Bulldog Lane. "I'm not sure, but we can check it out for ourselves. The girl's soccer team has a practice today, so the locker room is robably open."

"I don't want to go back there!"

"You have to. It's the only way you'll believe it isn't any of the people who care about you."

The red truck parked outside the gym. A blue sedan pulled in next to them, Officer Fax Parker and FBI agent Jack Sigety emerged from within.

"What are you two doing?" Max came around to the driver's side. "I told you, Louis, to bring Penny straight home."

'I know, but we have an English exam next week in Mr. Learner's class. Penny left her literature book in her gym locker. I just brought her here to pick it up."

Penny couldn't believe Louis lied. She noticed Max turning his attention to her.

"Is that true, young lady?" Max questioned.

She crossed her fingers. "Yes, it will only take a second."

"We'll escort you."

Max opened the truck door and Louis rushed to Penny's side. "You need help."

"No, I'm feeling better." She stepped down and strolled with him inside the gym with the two officers of the law following behind.

Louis put his hand on the door. "Wait a minute. What if there's a girl changing in there?"

"That's what got us in this mess in the first place." Max cracked the door open and checked. "All clear."

The four of them went in. Penny's heart was in her throat. Feeling it pound, she moved closer to her locker. She turned the combination into her lock, clicked it, then swung open the door. No books were inside, only a few jerseys and a pair of cleats. "I must have left the book at home after all."

She tried not to remember the last time she was here. But her mind immediately flashed back to her attack and the sounds of the footsteps. She recalled a click and then a slide, almost as if the person had some kind of limp. Her hands flew to her ears. Tears came to her eyes. She turned around, shaking and staring upward. There it was with Max Parker and Jack Sigety standing underneath, the vent.

It couldn't have been more than one and half feet across, maybe one foot wide. Much smaller than she remembered, horror mixed with some weird sense of relief washed over her.

"Are you okay?" Max came forward and put his arm around her. "Let's get you out of here."

Together the four of them left the locker room and returned to their vehicles. Penny didn't say a word when Louis started the engine.

"No Bulldogs could fit through that," Louis commented.

Penny leaned back into the seat feeling more comfortable now that she was outside. She lifted one of her legs and placed her foot on top of the opposite knee. "You're right, Frank or Gordan couldn't have either."

She slapped her tennis shoe and felt a string hanging from its sole. She took a better look. A single stand. Could this be part of a duckweed root? Did this come from the hospital or from the floor of the locker room, she wondered?

"Your shoe's untied." Louis told her.

"Has anyone been fishing at Catfish Pond lately?"

Louis raised a brow. "Catfish Pond is too polluted to fish anymore, Penny. Besides fried Catfish sucks."

"What about Cyress Swamp?"

"Airboat Willy's closed down after some kid got killed a few years back. It's too dangerous in the swamp with all the gators. I don't know anyone who goes there for anything." He scratched his chin. "Although, with all the duckweed, duck hunters might shoot migrating birds there occasionally."

"It's illegal to duck hunt this time of the year." Penny's hand clutched over the string.

"What's all this about?"

"The kid that died at Airboat Willy's— when was that?"

"Right before Dante and I started high school. We had made plans to go to Airboat Willy's. Then there was some big article in the paper about some kid falling out the second story window onto the deck. The kid's parents sued for millions and Kevin Willy hit the road faster than santa Claus on Christmas Eve."

Penny wondered. "Do you think the library would have a copy of that article?"

"Probably, on microfilm. Why?"

"Take me to the library now."

Louis shook his head no. "Uncle Max will yell at me again."

"Who are you more afraid of me or him?"

Louis laughed. "Okay, but if I didn't like you, I certainly wouldn't be ticking off the police."

"What are they going to do, arrest us for wanting a better education?"

He checked the rearview mirror. "They're tailing us closer now."

"Can we lose them?"

"No way, not in this rust bucket."

"Then we'll tell them we're doing research for that English test. They'll believe it. Go to the Satellite Beach Library; it's not that far."

The red truck passed the Margarita house and continued straight toward the intersection leading to Satellite Beach. "They're flashing lights." Louis informed. "They want us to pull over!"

Penny saw the red light on the blue sedan's dash in the sideview mirror. "Keep going."

Speeding through the intersection, Louis drove several more blocks then turned down Cassia Street. The large square building with the Dolphin statue out front was only a few feet away.

The sedan pulled in next to the truck. "Stop!" Screamed Jack Sigety. Louis turned into the parking lot of the "Satellite Beach Public Library."

Max Parker slowed his car then jumped out. With his hands on his hips, his eyes were glaring at Louis. "Now what?"

Louis pointed to her. "She made me."

Chapter 12

Max extended his hand to Penny. "Take this." He said. "If you're not going to cooperate with us, at least you can keep this with you at all times so we can find you if there's a problem."

Penny took the familiar FBI tracking and signaling device. "I left this in the locker room that night. I tried to reach for the box but I was hit on the arm before I could. What good is this thing if you can't get to it?"

"We made the black SR27 more sensitive. We can also switch it on manually now and locate you whenever we feel the need."

"That's very important," Max reminded. "Since you don't seem to want to go where you're supposed to."

Penny got out of the truck and headed for the library entrance. "Louis and I have a few things to look up for our test. It won't take long."

"The library has many aisles and different rooms." Agent Sigety gave his opinion. "It could be dangerous."

Max kept up with her pace. "I'll keep her in my sight."

The sliding door opened and the four of them walked into the quiet study area with the computer desks.

"Why don't you and Agent Sigety wait here?" Penny smiled. "We'll just be in that room over there or at the reference desk." She pointed to the room with glass windows. Inside was a typewriter and the microfilm machine.

Jack Sigety nodded. "We'll be watching."

"Sure." She took Louis by the hand, leading him through a row of bookshelves to the reference desk. They stood in the back of the two person line to speak to the librarian.

"Why don't you just ask Uncle Max about Cypress Swamp? He probably knows all about the case."

"I can't," Penny explained. "He'll ask too many questions. It's better this way."

"What are you looking for?"

"I have a hunch and if I'm right I might be able to solve who's kidnapping all those girls."

Louis pressed. "You should tell them who you think it is!"

"They won't listen to me."

"Why not? Maybe they'll even help prove your idea."

"And if it doesn't pan out like Gordan's van?"

"They'll think you're even more crazy." Louis understandingly said.

A thin man with shoulder length blonde air leaned over the desk and asked. "May I help you?"

Penny informed him of the dates ranging in the two weeks in August, three years ago. "I need them in microfilm."

"Which paper?"

Louis answered for her. "Florida Today"

"Sign in." The man gave Penny a sheet.

She filled in her name and date.

"How long will you need the machine?"

"Not longer than an hour." Penny handed him back his pen.

"There is a half hour limit."

"Okay" Penny and Louis followed him to the glass room.

He shoved a key into the door and said. "My assistant will bring what you need."

They hurried in and sat down in front of the large black monitor.

"Do you know how to use this?" Penny asked Louis.

He pointed to a slot. "Yes, you put the film here. Then you press this green button and it feeds automatically."

"It would probably be in the local section."

The door reopened and a chubby older woman wearing a Rockledge High T-shirt came in with a shoe box. "Two weeks worth of papers." She tossed the box down and walked away.

"She was real helpful." Louis said sarcastically.

"No kidding." Penny took the first reel of film out of a round plastic container "Stick it, here, right?"

"Yup." He helped her, then pressed the button.

A blue light flashed on with the date.

"One page per frame." Louis continued to hit the green button. "Tell me when you see the local section."

"There it is, stop."

Penny searched. "Not this one."

Louis hit the red button and caught the film as it spun out. "Try the next."

She got the second reel and began again. "Local section, no not this one either."

For several more reels they repeated this process until she found what she was looking for. There it is, "Trouble at the Swamp."

Penny studied the small picture of Airboat Willy's, a two story wooden structure built in the center of four horizontally grown Cypress trees. A large deck had been constructed above the green water. Several large airboats were tied up in the front. "Wow, Airboat Willy's is really spooky."

"It used to be a cool hang out for Dante and me. We'd eat gator for lunch in the upstairs diner, then airboat the rest of the afternoon over the swamp."

"How'd you get there?"

"The fishing Boat, not "Eau Girl." Your Dad's boat is too big. Small boats or canoes can tie up off the back deck."

Penny began to read the article. "The Indialantic Police Department is investigating an accident at Airboat Willy's where a young man reportedly fell out of the second story window. The cause is still being determined." Penny skimmed down to the second paragraph and continued out loud. "The young man is hospitalized at Regional Hospital with a broken hip and arm. He is said to be in stable condition."

"He didn't die?" Louis sat up. "I thought that he had."

"There's no name."

"He was a juvenile. They never print a name if the person's under age."

"The police are currently searching for Kevin Willy, owner of Airboat Willy's. He disappeared soon after the young man's parents filed a lawsuit. Penny stood. "It keeps describing the person who got hurt as a young man. He could be a teenager!"

"So?'

"We've got to go to the swamp."

Louis hit the red button and wrapped up the reel. "No way, that's way too risky."

"We have to solve this case on our own. The cops won't believe me. And you know it."

"Maybe you should concentrate on the Championship and let the FBI and Uncle Max figure out who the criminals are."

Penny closed the reel container. "There won't be a Championship game for me if he isn't caught. Don't you get it. I can't play. I could walk out onto that field and get shot from any seat in the stadium or be attacked afterwards. All he has to do is pick the right quarter or a specific press conference. The Bulldog's schedule will be publicized. If I surprise him now, he's got to play by my rules."

"The FBI will be coming to the Championship. They can protect you."

"They were there the last time, remember? They couldn't keep me safe then."

Louis got up and sighed. "Who do you think it is?"

"I don't want to say yet, not until I'm sure. Just, please, help me. You're the only person I trust. I've got to do this. I have to or that monster is going to take my dream of being a Champion away from me."

He embraced her. "All right, tell me the game plan."

"The first thing we've got to do is lose Uncle Max and Agent Sigety."

Chapter 13

Penny carried her balloons and flowers from the truck to the front door of her house. She glanced over her shoulder to Louis, then to the police car parking by the mailbox.

"I think we should ask Dante to come along," Louis said.

"He might rat on us."

Louis disagreed. "Dante loves excitement. He'll go anywhere for a thrill."

Penny opened the front door. Arms immediately swung out for her. Her mother began kissing her cheek. Her father lifted her off the ground in a big hug.

"Surprise!" Her parents yelled.

Penny noticed that the living room had been decorated with blue and gray streamers. Balloons hung from the ceiling in a big net. Against the glass patio door, tables were covered with white cloths. Sitting in the middle was a Bulldog paw-shaped cake.

"We're throwing you a welcome home party!" Dr. Margarita exclaimed.

She tried to sound excited. "Great."

"We thought that you might want to be with your friends tonight," her mother said. "The police let us know they ruled the Bulldogs out as suspects."

"Yes, I know."

"We wanted to take your mind off things." Dr. Margarita wrapped his arms around her. "What do you think of the decorations?"

"They're beautiful, Dad."

Louis added. "It must have taken you forever to blow up all those balloons."

"I just stopped." Dr. Margarita patted his chest. "How are you, Son?"

"Well, Sir, and you?"

"Better now that our daughter's home." Dr. Margarita squeezed Penny's cheeks.

"Are you hungry, Honey?" her mother asked.

"No, Penny replied. "Is Dante here?"

"Sis!" Dante leaned his head over the railing upstairs.

Louis headed toward him. Penny, wanting to hear Dante's response, excused herself. "I'm kind of tired, Mom. I'm just going to take a nap upstairs. Louis came to see Dante anyway."

"Are you too sleepy for a party?" Dr. Margarita wondered. "We could postpone it to tomorrow night?"

"What time does it start?"

"Seven o'clock," he replied.

"That leaves plenty of time to rest." Slowly, she paced herself upstairs to the end of the hallway where Dante and Louis were talking.

"Are you two nuts?" Dante snapped at them. Since Airboat Willy's closed down, the 'gators and snakes have taken over the swamp. They're no longer being hunted."

"Please help us." Penny insisted.

Dante leaned his muscular frame against the wall. "You really think you know who hurt you?"

'I'm not sure."

"How are you going to hide from Max Parker and that FBI agent?" Dante wondered. "What about Mom and Dad?"

"We'll sneak out your bedroom window with that ladder you have, the fire ladder," Penny suggested. "Then we'll run to the boathouse, lower the fishing boat into the water and sail out. No one will ever know we're leaving."

"Won't the cops hear the boat engine turning on, Sis?"

"Not over the cars on South Patrick road."

Dante shook his head. "I don't think you should try this. Louis and I will check out the swamp with the cops and see if there's anyone there. You stay in the house so Mom and Dad won't worry. They've been through enough lately."

"No!"

"The swamp is no place for a girl!"

"Says who?"

"Sis, be reasonable. Louis, say something!"

Louis shrugged. "I think she'll be fine."

Dante opened his bedroom door, went to his closet, pulled out the ladder off the top self and turned to the open window. With a big thrust, he tossed the ladder out, making sure it was secured to the ledge. "You two have ten minutes."

"What?" Penny gasped.

"If that creep is in the swamp, you'll need backup, people with guns. I'll wait awhile, then I'll tell the cops you're not in the house anymore. I'll also cover for you with Mom and Dad. Just be back in time for the party."

"What's the story for Mom and Dad?"

"If they notice you're not in your room, I'll say you two went for ice cream and they were too busy putting the party together to hear you leave." Penny strolled to Dante's side and smiled, "Thanks." "I would come but somebody's got to stay here and make sure you both don't get into too much trouble."

She "handed him the flowers and balloons. Leaving the FBI beeper on the floor, she reached for the rope ladder. "Give us at least ten minutes."

"I will, but you should take that with you."

Louis rushed over and grabbed the FBI beeper. "Dante's right. The cops should know exactly where we are in case your hunch is right. Uncle Max can use the signal to track us in the swamp. Let's go."

"If we leave it, we'll have more time to search for the kidnapper."

"All the more reason why we need it." He stuck the FBI beeper in his jeans and scooted out the window.

Penny followed. Going down the rope ladder was easier than she had thought. Each step she took with care, descending to the ground from the second story. As soon as her feet touched the earth, she began jogging after Louis to the boathouse at the end of the short dock behind the house. Louis removed the tarp off the top of the small fishing boat and with its pulley lowered the seven footer into the water with a loud splash.

"Careful," he warned her.

Penny cautiously stepped into the boat and sat in the middle. "I'm in." She grasped her seat, feeling the current rock the boat

He jumped into the back and started the engine.

Together the two of them glided out of the boathouse into the dark blue Indian River.

Penny watched the water spraying over the side. "It's rough today."

"The swamp won't be." It's like death there, nothing moves but the evil creatures."

Penny turned her head back and saw Dante standing in the window, his hand outstretched. She waved back, secretly hoping he would keep his word. They needed time to get away.

Chapter 14

Louis couldn't have been more right about wicked animals lurking in the swamp. The bellow of the alligators made her shiver as the boat entered into the darkness of the cypress trees. She didn't see any of the cold-blooded reptiles, but hearing their raucous calls, she knew they couldn't be far.

In Florida's mild winter the thick cypress lose their leaves, but the trees still consume the sky with their thick moss-covered branches blocking out much of the sunlight. Her eyes trailed down their gray-brown trunks to the Cypress knees, the strange part of the tree that grows up and around the ground wing in crooked shapes, reminding her of a witch's broom handle.

Below, the murky water was covered with algae and duckweed. Penny reached down with a finger to scoop some up. Her index skimmed over a slippery skin atop the water. The head of a snake popped up.

"Don't put your hands in," Louis warned.

Watching the long snake zig zag away on top of the water, Penny questioned. "Was it poisonous?"

"Yes, a water moccasin. They eat fish."

"People too?"

He chuckled, "Only if they're really hungry."

With two ways for the boat to turn, right or left, Penny wondered if Louis knew which way to go. Before she could even ask, the boat began making a right, further into the water hyacinths.

"No owls out today," Louis mentioned, matter-of-factly.

Penny stared upward into the trees again where osprey and vultures were crouched high in the dead branches, shading their young. Their heads followed the boat, pivoting slowly.

She didn't understand, "Is there something wrong with owls?"

"It's rumored that if you hear a glade owl hoot during the day, it's a sign of death approaching."

Every duckweed began looking like a snake; each bullfrog croak sounded like an alligator; each tree seemed to come alive and reach out for her. Penny gasped, "How far is it to Airboat Willy's?"

"Not far."

"Good."

"Are you scared?" he asked over the roar of the motor.

Penny, smelling the rotting vegetation in the oppressive, humid air, answered sarcastically. "No, I love it here. We should come to the swamp more often."

A mother duck paddled in front of the boat with a brood of four ducklings trailing behind in a line. The sight of this colorful family relaxed Penny a bit. She admired their brown feathers and their bright green and orange heads gobbling down the duckweed. In the midst of the dark waters, at least some of the creatures seemed beautiful and at peace. "Aw, look at the babies, Louie. They're so cute and cuddly, especially the tiny one at the end?"

Suddenly a giant gray head appeared with mouth agape, snapped over the last duckling before her eyes, then resubmerged quietly.

The gator's snout seemed to be as big as the boat bow to Penny. She screamed.

"It's all right. They can't get in the boat." Louis said.

The mother duck sounded a soft covey call, scurrying the rest of her ducklings to the safety of a fallen log with resurrection fern festooned in its crumbling bark.

"Did you see that?" Penny asked. "The baby was right there and then, it was gone."

Louis sped the boat up and made another turn left. Zebra butterflies floated past, airing their damp black and white wings. In the undergrowth of ferns, brown turtles lumbered, extending their heads to snap at their mosquito prey.

" Airboat Willy's," Louis pointed ahead.

Penny saw the structure coming closer. Perched onto four horizontal fallen cypress trees was a two-story wooden structure made out of cypress wood. A dock had been built below it with stairs that led to the front door. The falling sign above the doorway announced Airboat Willy in faded red letters. Spanish moss completely covered the roof and was inching down the walls.

"I don't see any other boats, Penny."

She remembered that Louis had told her of another dock behind Airboat Willy's. "We should go to the back and make sure that no one is on the other side."

"The fences are missing."

"What fences?" Penny inquired.

"There used to be a barbed wire fence around the dock to keep out the critters."

Louis steered the boat around the building. He immediately tied the boat up to a rickety post on the dock. "Let's hurry." He shut down the engine, stepping onto the algae-covered dock. "I doubt anybody is here."

Penny noticed that there were no other Jon-boats or airboats. "Do you think the cops took Willy's airboats to pay for that injury lawsuit?" She took Louis' hand, lifting herself out of the boat onto the dock.

"Maybe."

Cautiously, she moved onto the slimy boards. Falling into that murky water seemed to be a fate worse than death. Hand in hand, they walked around the building to the front stairs where Louis stopped.

"What is it?"

Louis didn't answer her.

She heard a hissing sound, and froze. At the top of the stairs was a six foot gator with four shot legs, greenish-gray bumpy skin and thin spiked tail. Its elongated mouth looked as if it were grinning at them. Countless piercing shards of teeth showed the hanging flesh of a previous dinner.

"Back up," he said.

Penny's foot lowered to the step below. Quickly moving backwards, Louis accidentally gave her a shove. She slipped and fell down the stairs, tumbling into the dark water.

"Penny!" Louis cried out.

Her head bobbed up. "Help!" The water stirred around her. Pairs of eyes popped up from three different directions, gator eyes with catlike slits for pupils. "Help!" she screamed again in terror.

He hopped down to the dock edge and reached out his hand. Penny grabbed it and he lifted her back to the surface, helping her onto the dock.

"I'm okay," she gratefully smiled.

Louis picked her up just before a smaller four-foot gator slid onto the deck. With his sneakers slipping and sliding beneath him, Louis carried her quickly to the other side. He turned around; the gator hadn't followed them. Gently, he put her down. "We've got to get out of the swamp before we become gator food."

She noticed a window in the back of Airboat Willy's. "Let me check if anyone's inside first. That's why we came here, isn't it?"

Louis got into the boat and started the engine. "No one could live in this place anymore."

Carefully, Penny stood on her tiptoes to peer inside. What she saw made her mouth drop, her eyes bulge. In a semicircle, six women sat huddled together in the middle of the wooden floor with their hands tied behind their backs. Their bodies were wet with perspiration as they leaned heavily against one another for support. She recognized the one closest to the window. Ebony skinned Alexandra Martin still had corn rows in her hair. On her chest, the number 41 decorated her Florida State basketball jersey.

"The other girls!" Penny announced excitedly.

Louis stopped the engine. "What?

"One through Six, we found them!"

Quickly, he jumped out of the boat and bounded to her side. "You were right?"

"Yes, this is the Number Kidnapper's hideout!"

Unbelieving, he looked for himself, then embraced her. "Now all we've got to do is figure out a way inside to free them."

Loud hissing and grunting noises began filling the air. The familiar sound made them shudder in each other's arms. In unison, they turned their heads to see gator after gator scrambling aboard the dock.

Chapter 15

Each bumpy beast lumbered toward them with nail-tipped claws. Slowly, the alligators began surrounding Louis and Penny. One took a step closer, then grunted. Penny saw an orange tipped brown feather clinging to its snout just like the baby duckling's colors. "Not you!"

Louis yanked the FBI beeper out of his jeans pocket. "I'll signal the cops." He pressed the red button repeatedly.

"It's a little late for that." Penny grabbed a moss-covered cypress tree branch and pulled, trying to break it off.

"Go eat some fish, you ugly monsters!" Louis threw the beeper at the closest gator and it bounced off his snout.

"Help me!" Penny alerted.

Louis, seeing what she was doing, grabbed onto the branch with her and tore off a limb.

"Keep it," she said.

Immediately he swung the limb out in front of them, trying to scare off the gators.

More were coming out of the water. Louis had to hit one with stick on the tip of the snout before it lunged back.

"The window!" Remembering a way to escape, Penny broke off a smaller branch and swung at the glass.

With a loud crash, the window shattered.

"You got me!" Louis yanked a small piece of glass out of his forearm.

She gasped, "Get into the building quick!"

The gators hissed louder, lurching back and forth as the smell of blood excited them. Stumbling over one another, the reptiles inched closer.

"You first!" Louis ordered.

"No!" Penny shoved him against the wall and began lifting him up. Louis grabbed onto the window ledge and pulled himself in.

Hearing the women scream inside, Penny jumped up. She tried to lift herself over the sill but before she could, she felt a strong tug at her leg. She pranced down in horror to find a gator latching onto her jeans' leg.

"One's got my pants!"

Louis wrapped his arms around her shoulders to stop her from falling back down. The gators were gathering below her feet with their jaws wide open. "I don't want to die!" She cried out.

Lifting his hands to the belt buckle on her jeans, Louis pulled. The gator didn't let go, only stood on his back two feet, balancing himself with his tail. "Grab my neck tight!"

Penny did as he instructed.

With this added leverage he raised her a few inches higher, yanking the gator off the ground.

His arms were shaking from the weight. Penny knew she had to help or his muscles would give out. She released one hand and pushed on the side of the window. Struggling for a better hold, the reptile opened his jaw but seemed to lose his balance at the same time. He flopped back onto the dock with a loud thud.

Louis and Penny fell on top of one another on Airboat Willy's floor, then paused to catch their breaths.

"Untie us!" a voice demanded.

"Thank God," said another.

Penny rose to her feet and ran over to the six women, recognizing most of them. Karin Dubin, the Olympic gymnast gazed up at her with frightened eyes. Her hair was matted from dried blood and her leg was black and blue. Next to Karin sat the hockey player from Alabama, Cindy Cambell. Penny noticed that her pretty dark-complected face had been beaten, but the bruises had turned yellow and were healing.

To the right of Cindy sat Janis Teller, the soccer player from South Carolina. Her big thighs were known nationwide for her over-the-head Kicks.

Next to Janis, Dawn Kresil trembled. She looked as beautiful as ever with her long, sandy hair and well-defined arms; Dawn was Georgia State's leading softball pitcher.

On the floor by Dawn crouched a woman who still had grease on her face and oil on her plain, brown jumpsuit. "Are you that racecar driver?"

"Yes, Wendy Hamilton." She answered. "Who are you?"

"Penny."

The last and tallest of them all was Alexandra Martin, number 41, the basketball player from Florida State. Louis dropped down to his knees and began unwrapping the square knots behind Alexandra's back.

When she was free, Alexandra helped untie Janis Teller. "What do you two want with us?"

Louis responded. "Where here to help."

Penny leaned over and untied the ropes from around Karin's hands. Karin in turn released Dawn's wrists. One by one the girls found their freedom. Cindy, Dawn, Janis, Wendy and Alexandra moved slowly to the empty bar at the corner of the log-lined room, stretching their legs.

Still seated on the floor, Karin rubbed her arms and sked. "Do you know who did this to us?"

Penny looked over the room. All that remained of Willy's furniture were two lopsided stools. "I'm like you. I was his number eight but I escaped."

"Number eight?" Karin shrugged. "What are you talking about?"

"It doesn't matter now." Louis took off his shirt and wrapped up his bleeding forearm. "We're surrounded by gators. We can't leave."

"The guy with the limp feeds them." Wendy explained. "They're always close."

"We better find a way out and quick." Alexandra reminded. "The sun will be going down soon."

"He comes back every day at sunset." Janis added.

"But the dock is full of gators," Penny announced. "We're stuck here until the cops come."

"Oh, no we're not." Alexandra Martin shot up the stairs, taking two at a time. A few seconds later she returned holding a long stick with a cattle prod on the end. "This will work. I've seen him use this when he's mad at them."

Louis took it. "Can all of you make it through the window?"

Karin nodded no from the floor. "My leg is broken."

"Then we'll all take the long way," Penny announced.

Cindy Cambell assisted Karin to the door by having the injured gymnast lean on her like a human crutch. The other four trailed behind Cindy, making sure if Karin fell she would be caught. Penny went behind the lot to protect the group from the rear.

"We'll move slowly," Louis opened the door.

The six foot gator that Penny and Louis had seen resting at the top of the stairs, turned around and hissed. Louis swung out the prod but before it even connected, the gator backed away and crawled down into the water.

"I think they know this thing," he concluded.

Swinging the weapon out in front of the girls, Louis descended the stairs. As soon as the prod came near the reptiles on the dock, they hustled back into the water. Each of the gators retreated amazingly fast for being such huge creatures.

Penny realized Louis was right. The Numbers Kidnapper must have used this on the gators. They were conditioned to know that it would hurt if they got hit.

Half way around the deck, on the side of Airboat Willy's, Penny saw a gator crawling back up, heading for the back of the group. "Throw it to me!" Louis tossed Penny the prod and she waved it at the snarly animal. Immediately, the reptile slid back into the dark water.

"Here!" Louis yelled.

Penny returned the prod to him, just in time to scare another charging one from snapping at his legs.

When the group reached the boat, they found a passenger already in it, the largest gator they'd seen, a ten footer. Louis shook the prod. The giant cocked his head, seemed to challenge Louis, and stared back, unafraid.

"I thought you said they couldn't get in a boat." Penny reminded.

Louis showed the cattle prod to the creature again. "Guess, I was wrong."

Quickly, the reptile moved to the side, opened his mouth full of four inch long teeth.

Louis roared, "Go home, you dinosaur reject!"

The gator attacked, jumping midair. With the prod, Louis hit it underneath the chin. Sparks flew and the reptile dropped motionlessly onto the deck.

"Everyone into the boat before this monster wakes back up." He said.

A faint buzzing noise came echoing through the trees, a humming noise like an airplane.

Dawn screamed in terror. "The Kidnapper's coming back!"

"That could be the police in an airboat." Louis stated.

One by one the girls crammed into the Jon-boat two on each small seat and the rest stuffing themselves into the bottom like sardines into a can. The second they were all aboard, Louis restarted the engine.

"Wait!" Penny jumped back onto the deck, leaped over the gator and grabbed the FBI beeper. "If it's not the police, they'll still need to track us."

"Come back!" Louis ordered her.

The long gator's tail moved. She stepped over the twitching limb and reentered into the boat.

With a mighty hiss, the big gator woke and swung around to stare at those who had stunned him.

Chapter 16

Louis maneuvered the boat away from the dock before the gator could snap his powerful jaws at them.

Hearing his low, hair-raising hiss, Penny glanced back and saw a bleeding line on the bottom of the gator's snout. "That prod mark is going to leave a scar."

"Catch you later, Alligator." Louis yelled.

After a few hundred yards, the engine started sputtering; the boat began losing speed and dipping in the swam water.

Alexandra cried. "The engine's dying!"

Louis steered the boat behind a giant cypress log which was covered in ferns, and shut off the motor just as it began spewing out bluish-gray smoke.

"What are we going to do?" Penny gasped, watching the gator with the wounded neck slip back into the water. "We're dead if we stay out here!"

"With eight people, we'll take on water once we hit the river current. The waves would fill this boat in no time. It's Weighing down. The engine's failing because we're too heavy. We'll drown out there. Our only choice is to hide and wait until the police show up."

Raising her head, Cindy responded, "It will get dark soon."

"What if the cops don't come until morning?" Karin asked, trying to keep her leg straight.

"Maybe we should go back to Airboat Willy's," Louis said, "and fight this guy."

"He carries a gun." Cindy warned.

Louis stabbed a cypress root and tied the boat to a knob sticking out of it. "Then we'll stay here until the police arrive. It may be in the morning but that still gives a better chance of staying alive than having to swim miles to Indialantic." He glanced at Karin and noticed her face wincing in pain.

"Can't we make it to the shoreline right outside the swamp?"

"We'd be in plain sight," Louis pointed out.

The sound of the airboat grew louder. Penny didn't know if she should rejoice or be afraid. "I hope that's Uncle Max."

With the tree about a half foot higher than his head, Louis stretched to peer around it. A furry raccoon jumped out at him from inside. Surprise, Louis gasped, and the masked critter scurried up a nearby cypress tree.

"Quiet!" reminded Wendy.

"Maybe he won't look for us since it's getting dark," Janis added.

Penny hoped. "Yeah, maybe."

A small hulled boat with a steel metal fan mounted in the back skimmed across the top of the water toward Airboat Willy's. The teenage driver, wearing black boots, blue shirt and a gun tucked into a pair of dark slacks, flipped a switch next to the seat. The giant fan whirled to a stop, allowing the airboat to glide in toward the back of the dock.

From the driver's seat, the young man hopped down into the hull and started tying the airboat to the rickety pole. All of a sudden, he stopped and limped over to the broken window, dragging his left leg.

"He knows they're gone now," Penny whispered as she watched him.

After a few minutes of his peering through the opening, he turned around. Penny saw his face: a solid jaw, big deep-set blue eyes and short military cut light brown hair. He was a lot taller than Penny had thought, and more muscular.

"Do you recognize him?" Penny whispered to Louis.

"No."

"Are you sure you don't?" she repeated.

Louis took another peek around the trunk and sunk back. "No, I've never seen him before. He looks awfully big, though, to fit in an air conditioning duct."

"He's skinny enough," Penny added after a pause.

"Why do you think I'd recognize him?" Louis asked.

Overhearing, Alexandra leaned closer and inquired, "Do you know who he is, Penny?"

"I think he could be Kerry McLoy."

"You mean McLoy -related to Gordan McLoy?" Louis seemed confused.

"Yes, he's his brother."

He frowned. "Gordan doesn't have a brother, only a sister."

Penny took another look. The young man hobbled back into the airboat, untied the ropes, and clicked on the loud fan. He grabbed the rudder stick in front of the high seat and steered the boat away, toward the swamp's entrance.

"He's searching for us." Wendy guessed.

"He won't find anything there," Penny stated, "except maybe the cops."

Louis waited until the airboat noise had died down and then pulled Penny close with blood seeping through the shirt wrapped around his forearm onto her wet T-shirt. "Are you sure? Gordan's never even mentioned he had a brother to me."

"Would Dante know Kerry?"

"I doubt it," Louis answered. "or I would have heard of him by now."

"Hey, I hate to interrupt," Cindy said. "I don't really care who that psycho is right now; I'd just like to make it out of this swamp in one piece. If you haven't noticed, this boat is beginning to take on water."

Penny looked down to see the duckweed and algae water washing in over the sides of the overloaded boat. "Cup it out," she quickly ordered.

"I can't swim," Wendy alerted the crew.

Over Penny's shoulder, Louis comforted by adding, "Don't worry, we should be able to keep the water from flooding the boat."

Penny rechecked the beeper. The light was flashing, so she pressed the button again. "I hope Uncle Max finds us before Kerry does."

"Why are you so sure he is this Kerry fellow?" Dawn asked her.

"I'm not. But his brother Gordan did leave duckweed on my hospital room floor."

"Gordan?" Louis shrugged. "Do you think he was involved in this too?"

"He came to the swamp, Louis; there's no doubt about that. It was either Frank or Gordan. Frank is an only child and doesn't have many friends except for those on the team. Gordan has a brother no one seems to ever have seen. It's more likely to be Gordan's relative -that's my guess."

"I don't understand."

"Indialantic is a small town; everybody knows everybody, right, Louie?"

"Yeah, so?"

"Nobody knows Kerry. Sarah told me she has another brother. You've never heard anyone even talk about him. Don't you think that's strange?"

"Maybe he goes to another school," Louis surmised.

"He certainly appears to be close to our age. Why would he if he lives in this district, unless he attends that special school for handicapped kids?" Penny figured, "Don't you see? He got hurt in the swamp and he's taking it out on us."

"Why?" Wendy pressed.

"I'm not clear on that yet." Penny responded. "Did any of you see a really tall guy hanging around Airboat Willy's? His hair is sandy colored and kind of wild like a mop."

The girls all looked at one another.

"I heard someone else talking to Kerry outside," Janis admitted, "but I didn't see him."

"We all got knocked out when we were kidnapped. None of us saw anything but our hands tied up to each other when we woke up in this swamp hole," Alexandra reported.

The whirling fan of the airboat became louder. Penny shivered, "Kerry's coming back."

"Maybe he'll search the other path," Louis tried to sound hopeful.

"Everyone quiet." Penny put a finger to her lips to shush them.

Before the last word left her mouth, the airboat skimmed across the surface of the water and created a large wave which crashed to the fishing boat. Immediately the girls started scooping water out with their hands. Penny craned her neck to watch the airboat whiz by in the opposite direction.

"This boat is going to sink if he keeps passing us at that speed." Karin predicted.

Wendy started to weep. "I can't swim."

Penny reached out to hold her shoulder. "It's okay. We'd paddle the boat to Airboat Willy's before that could happen."

"You'd both become prisoners too then." Wendy warned.

"The FBI will save us eventually anyway," Penny tried to reassure her.

"Where are these cops and his Uncle Max you keep mentioning?" Janis shook her head. "They certainly aren't hurrying to get here."

"They probably had to find some airboats or jon-boats."

After scooping out nearly all the puddle from the boat, Penny leisurely rested her green coated hand over the side. "Great," Penny added sarcastically.

Louis grabbed her arm. "Be careful! Below us!"

Penny gazed over the side and saw an enormous alligator relaxing near the boat. He seemed to be waiting for one of them to make a mistake. Then she noticed the blood tinged water near his head. Staring back at her through yellow green eyes was their old nemesis. "It's Scarface!

Chapter 17

Louis raised the cattle prod beside him in the boat as he announced, "Scarface won't make a move, not with this on board."

Penny shifted between Alexandra and Louis, sitting back. "I just wanted to play football. How did I wind up in this mess?"

Karin moaned, grabbing her leg. The rocking of the boat was taking its toll on her injury.

"You play football?" Alexandra yanked a duckweed out of her corn rows. "That's odd for a chick."

"I'm the quarterback for the Indialantic Bulldogs."

"No kidding?" Cindy smiled. "I always wanted to try to be a linebacker but my father thought hockey would work out my aggression better."

Penny laughed. "Does it?"

"Oh yeah, last year in the Olympics I got to check this Swede halfway to the moon."

Janis gave her a high five. "You guys got the gold medal. I saw that game!"

Alexandra brushed some algae off to Karin's broken leg. "So how did you start getting into football?"

Penny, glad to get her mind off their situation, explained. "My brother David was a quarterback. When he was alive he'd take me out in the backyard and throw me the ball to warm up before games. He made me feel special like I was a part of the reason why he kept winning." Catching Karin's attention, Penny tried to distract her from her hurt leg. "He was the greatest quarterback the Bulldogs ever have seen, so good under pressure and accurate in his passes. His eye for finding holes went down in history of Indialantic. They called him the Comeback Kid. If the Bulldog's weren't winning, everyone could count on him to throw a long pass right into the endzone."

"Big man on campus," Louis recalled with admiration.

"David had this aura about him. You know when you see a celebrity and get this feeling that he is really important, like an astronaut or the President. Well, times that by ten and that's how I felt when I was near my brother."

Cindy smiled. "He must have been really cool."

"He dressed in the finest clothes and he had this walk that, man, you just couldn't help but be impressed."

"David wore this silver chain around his neck with a big football charm that had his number eight on it." Louis added. "When you were close to him it was right in your face, almost like a reminder that you'd better respect who you were talking to."

"You were eight, don't you?" Wendy asked Penny. "I have number six painted on the car for my Dad."

"Your Dad is a racecar driver?" Penny inquired.

"Daytona 500 winner two times."

"Good for you!" Penny sighed. "David never won a Championship. He was killed right before he was supposed to play in the big game, three weeks to the day, in fact. But that's okay. If I play in the State Championship on Friday, he does too. We're partners, he and I, dead or not."

"How'd David die if you don't mind my asking?" Karin pressed for more information.

Slowly, Penny began her story. "The night after the Bulldogs won the Regional game over Lakeland, two fullbacks threw a party to celebrate. Someone spiked the punch. My brother had some, too much I guess. According to witnesses at the party, he gave his car keys to Pierce Sumner. Pierce must have had too much to drink too because he slammed my brother's Mustang right into a metal light pole on Highway A1A right across from Paradise Beach. That's where my brother died."

Alexandra gently put her arm around Penny's shoulders. "That must have been tough having a brother like that and then have him taken away so suddenly, right in his prime."

"Do you have any other brothers?" Dawn inquired.

"Dante, but he's not worth much. He spends most of his spare time trying to get me angry.

Alexandra stated. "I'd probably pick on you, too, if I thought I could never compare."

Penny straightened in the boat, keeping away from the side. "What are you talking about, Alexandra?"

"You can call me, Alex," giving Penny permission to use her nickname "Have you given any thought to the fact your other brother might just be tired of living in David's shadow?"

"You think he's jealous," Louis realized, "don't you."

"I'm just stating things the way I see them."

"Dante never wanted me to play football at all."

"Of course not. How could he when part of your reason for playing is for David, a person he can't ever compete with for your attention because he's gone."

Penny disagreed. "No, he just doesn't like me much."

The airboat noise roared louder. Eight heads lowered at the same time in the boat.

"Is it Kerry?" Penny asked Louis after the quiet returned.

He quickly peeked around the tree branch. "I can't see anybody."

"What are those whizzing sounds that come and go?" Penny asked as she rose to peer around left and right. Both boating paths were clear.

"Do you see anything?" Cindy questioned.

Penny answered, "Nothing, but that loud buzz just starts and stops.

"Is there another boat path?" Karin asked Louis.

Louis pondered for a moment. "Only two for Jon-boats but an airboat can go on trails small fishing boats can't. When Dante and I used to come out here we took out Willy's airboats over the grassy bog on the other side of the swamp. It was the best fishing, plus with all the saw grass there were plenty of shady places. That's probably what he's doing, roving back and forth, going through all the tall weeds looking for the girls. We're hearing his engine."

"As long as it keeps him busy," Janis smiled.

Next to the boat, bubbles began rising to the surface of the water, slowly breaking through the algae. Suddenly, two large yellow-green slit eyes rose and stared right at Penny.

"Scarface!" Penny tried to move to the other side of the boat.

Louis grabbed her. "He's just coming up for air. Relax."

Water sprayed from the gator's nostrils. His bumpy tail slapped across the surface. Finally, the enormous reptile sank to the bottom.

Penny exhaled deeply in relief. "He's down again."

Karin groaned, holding her leg. "Please don't move too much."

"I'm sorry," Penny apologize.

Louis kissed Penny's cheek. "Don't be scared. I've got the prod, remember?"

"So are you two boyfriend and girlfriend?" Alexandra questioned Penny and Louis.

Louis didn't answer.

Penny wondered why. She wanted to be his girlfriend, but didn't want to admit to anyone that he hadn't asked her. "We're dating."

"You make a cute couple," Dawn commented.

Louis agreed. "We do make that, don't we?"

Karin interrupted. "So what ever happened to the guy driving your brother? Did he die too?"

"No, Pierce plays for a college team now. He got a scholarship and somehow the vehicular homicide charge got reduced to driving under the influence."

"Rumor has it Coach Lambart, the Coach before ours, had something to do with that, but my Dad couldn't prove it."

Alexandra surmised. "I've heard of stuff like that happening, benefits of the program so to speak."

"Pierce was fined and got one year probation. He got off too easy."

"You play so your brother won't be forgotten?" Janis asked, "Don't you?"

Penny shrugged. "In a way, but I play because I love the game."

"You sound like a commercial," chuckled Karin. "That's so cliché. Is it true?"

"I enjoy shoving defenders away, knocking them to the ground, making them eat dirt."

"Now you're talking," Cindy the hockey player said understandingly.

Louis leaned closer to Penny in the boat, releasing the cattle prod from his fingers. "You too are scary," he chuckled.

"Try speeding over two hundred and fifty miles an hour," Wendy admitted. "The thrill is like nothing in this world."

"How about kicking a goal over your head from mid field?" Janis crossed her arms, staring at a six-inch green turtle climbing on top of the decaying log next to her.

"None of that can match trying to catch a ball that's been thrown fifty or more yards and hear that crowd grow silent wondering if I'm going to be able to pull it in," Louis held out his hands as he spoke. "And if you do, it's like the fourth of July and Christmas rolled into one."

"My Dad says sports are tests of the human spirit." Quietly Wendy added, " Of course he never attempted living out in a swamp. He should be more worried about me now than he ever was when I raced."

"We'll get home." Louis promised. "Just have some faith."

"Mom is probably starting to get mad at us for missing the bulldog's party." Penny recalled.

"No, if anything she's throwing the party to keep the Bulldogs out of trouble. So far it's not working for us." Louis raised a brow, looking at his steamed watch face. Besides, we won't even be late. Uncle Max will save us; he's never let us down yet."

Penny recalled when Max Parker caught the jewelry burglar who stole diamonds from the homes on Doctor's Row. "Louis is right, girls; we will be saved. My Uncle Max won't give up until he catches his crook."

Louis held up the FBI beeper and showed them all. "This is a signaling device that the police can use to track us. It lets them know our exact location."

Just then, the airboat started roaring toward them. Their heads lowered in unison and the girls huddled in the boat.

A plane couldn't have been louder, Penny thought. The sounds bounced off the trees. Several of the girls put their fingers in their ears. No one said anything because they all knew this time the airboat was heading toward Airboat Willy's.

A moment later, Penny took another gander around the side of the log. Sure enough, Kerry was docking the airboat in the back. After tying the boat to the rickety pole, he limped around the deck to the front door. "He's inside," Penny whispered the announcement.

No one spoke now. Having a conversation seemed no longer an option. Penny, along with the others, waited quietly for the signs that they would be rescued. In a sinking boat with a gator below, she clasped her hands together and prayed silently that they'd remain camouflaged from the Numbers Kidnapper.

The green, murky water began to change into a radiant orange as the sun set. Louis' hazel eyes gazed into Penny's. He reached out and kissed her cheek, tenderly. "We're magic, you and me." He reassured her, "We'll make it through this."

She gave him a halfhearted smile, "I hope so."

85

Chapter 18

"Kerry's got a spotlight." Louis softly announced to the group in the boat.

Penny squirmed in her seat so she could look for herself. Kerry was wearing a dark-colored hat with a flashlight attached. "Nightfall isn't going to stop him from searching for us."

A giant bullfrog jumped into her line of sight; the curious green amphibian sat there for a few minutes staring at her from the top of the cypress log. Louis tried to shoot it away but the frog snapped his long, thin tongue at his fingers. Immediately, Louis pulled his hand back. "It wants to eat me."

"Ribit."

"Go away," Penny whispered. "Shoo."

"Ribit."

Louis sneaked another peek around the side of the log. "Kerry's put the key in to start his engine. He'll be leaving soon."

The giant frog's attention moved to a transparent-winged dragonfly floating above. "Ribit, Ribit, Ribit." With lightning speed its tongue zapped out to capture his prey, gobbling it down in one giant gulp. "Ribit, Ribit."

"It's making too much noise." Alexandra said.

Penny, in agreement, grabbed the cattle prod to move the frog off its perch by gently poking its round, tan belly with the stick.

Recoiling, the frog rotated to face Airboat Willy's. "Ribit, Ribit, Ribit."

Instantly, the headlight flashed onto the nearby log with its amphibian guest. The passengers quickly ducked. Penny guessed that Kerry heard the racket and was making sure the girls weren't hiding in the surrounding ferns.

"Ribit."

She reached out to tap the frog again to move him into the water.

He didn't budge. His heavy body seemed to hardly feel Penny's finger. She repeated the effort. This time the amphibian inched forward.

"Ribit."

The spotlight from Kerry's hat didn't waver off the frog.

"Ribit, Ribit, Ribit," A butterfly flew by. The frog quickly leaped up, snatched the insect with his tongue and belly-flopped into the water with a big splash.

The engine of the airboat started. Penny gasped; Kerry might be coming closer to investigate. Within a few seconds the airboat was beside them, the head light beaming onto the Jon-boat.

"Drive to Airboat Willy's or I'll shoot!" ordered the voice. "Do it now."

Putting one hand over his eyes, Louis tried to see the face. "Who's there?"

Bang! A bullet shot into the water next to the boat.

Louis started the boat motor; one warning shot was enough to convince him to follow the voice's direction.

Two of the girls next to Penny started screaming. "He's going to kill us!"

"Don't do what he says!" yelled another.

With a smoking engine, Louis ignored their warnings and maneuvered them out from behind the log. "The police are on their way!" he announced.

The voice behind the light said, "No cop treads in this swamp."

At the front of Airboat Willy's, Louis docked the boat. Penny guessed that he chose there instead of in the back so that the police could see the Jon-boat easily when they entered from the river.

Dawn whimpered, "He said he'd kill us if we ever tried to escape!"

Louis jumped out to secure their line; Penny was next to step onto the dock.

The airboat glided in behind the Jon-boat. Kerry took off his hat and laid it on the driver's seat so he could watch everyone. His shadow limped toward them, reaching for the gun on his belt. "Number 8, I thought I'd seen the last of you."

"The FBI will be here soon. They're on the way." She hoped her voice didn't sound shaky.

Waving the gun over the group in the boat, he said. "Get up, all of you!"

One by one the girls crawled out of the Jon-boat. Louis walked over to stand in front of them. "You're making a big mistake," he warned the kidnapper.

"The way I see it, I've found more dinner for my pets."

Penny knew he was referring to the gators. "Did you ever think of keeping a dog?"

"A dog doesn't have as many teeth." He sounded amused. "Now get inside."

"I don't want to," Penny whined.

He lowered the gun towards her feet and fired. Penny jumped. The bullet went through the dock, missing her toes by only by a few inches.

Louis grabbed her. "What did she ever do to you?"

He coldly answered. "She was born."

"We know who you are!" Alexandra announced.

Taken back, he didn't say anything for a few moments. "Who gave you my name?"

"I did." Penny admitted. "You're Kerry McLoy, Gordan's brother."

He raised his head, not denying it, but said nothing.

"What are you going to do to us, Kerry?" Cindy asked while helping Karin out of the boat.

Karin yelled in pain, clutching her leg.

"You'll pay for disobeying me."

"Didn't you say that you needed to kidnap other girls before your plan could begin?" Janis tried to stall him.

"Seven's already dying in the hospital," Penny reported.

Moving closer to Penny, he shoved the gun into her chest. "You figured it out, didn't you, that I pick my victims by number?"

"Yes," she admitted.

Kerry wondered. "But do you know why?"

Trembling as the gun inched higher to her neck, she replied, "No." The barrel felt colder to her than the water, like ice against her skin. "Tell me."

"Nice try, but I don't think so."

An enormous gator slid onto the dock behind Kerry. Kerry turned halfway to greet him.

"Everyone, this is Godzilla, the baddest, meanest alligator in my swamp."

Blood began to trickle down the gator's neck. Immediately Kerry approached him and grabbed his snout. "What's this?"

Louis announced. "We nicknamed him Scarface."

Kerry let go of the enormous creature and limped back towards them. "Who did this to my gator?" His face was turning crimson with rage. "Answer me!"

"We had to push him away." Penny pointed down to the Jon-boat and showed them that they had taken his cattle prod. "He wanted to attack us."

Kerry aimed at the long stick, then shot expertly, dividing the prod into two parts. The bullet must have exited through the Jon-boat bottom because it began taking on water, slowly sinking. "Do you know what you did? My other pets will attack him once it gets dark. They'll smell his blood."

"Sorry." Penny grimaced.

"I'll have to keep him inside tonight." A smile inched across Kerry's full lips. "Maybe stay downstairs with all of you."

Karin moaned, leaning further into Cindy. "You don't have to kill us. We won't tell the police anything!"

"Sure, you won't. What do I look like, an idiot? Of course, you'll tell the cops. That's why I can't wait any longer for number nine." He swung the gun toward Penny. "Tonight, Quarterback, since you're so anxious, youi'll die first. I'll slice your chin and see how long you'll live out on the dock."

"What about Gordan?" Penny reminded. "Don't you want him here to help you finish the job?"

"Gordan isn't the mastermind."

"Then who is?" Penny interrogated.

Kerry began to shake with rage. "Just because I'm a cripple doesn't mean I don't have any brains!"

She tried to calm him. "Of course, you're smart and strong. I didn't mean it like that."

"Inside!" He motioned the gun back and forth.

Carefully, Cindy picked up Karin to carry her up the steps. Janis, Dawn, Wendy, Alexandra and Louis followed them into Airboat Willy's.

Penny waited, staring into Kerry's blue eyes. He wasn't handsome, but he didn't appear the way she had expected her kidnapper to look. His light brown hair was perfectly trimmed into a crew cut, his body was slim and dressed in stylish clothes, probably bought by the rich McLoy family.

Kerry could have easily taken the right road in life, she thought. Even after meeting him only a few minutes before, she almost had forgotten about his leg. He was able, willing and tough, hardly handicapped because of the power and vitality he possessed. Penny couldn't take her eyes off of him, wondering what made him tick. How could one accident turn a heart so cold?

"Get up the stairs!" Kerry raised his tone to Penny.

She took a step. Louis stood above watching intensely.

"If you have something to say, say it! It could be the last thing you ever do." Kerry snapped behind her.

Arriving at the top of the stairs, Penny turned around, "I feel sorry for you."

"Me too, Sherlock." Kerry slapped his hip. "Thanks to you women jocks, I amount to nothing."

"You're strong enough to kidnap us."

Kerry pushed her into Louis. "I was the greatest hockey player ever; now I can't even balance! You have no idea what it's like to be the best then lose it all."

Penny moved into Airboat Willy's with Louis standing in the open doorway. "It happened to my brother" she added softly.

"Shut up!" He shoved her again, harder than before.

Penny fell. As her body hit the wooden floor, her ears began to pick faint noises that sounded similar to Kerry's airboat, only louder. Kerry must have heard it too; he turned to the door, still holding the gun.

Wendy exclaimed. "The cops are coming!"

Kerry ran out to see, then slammed the door shut behind him.

Penny ran to the small front window and saw Kerry snap a padlock over the door's outside hinge. "He's locking us in!"

"Our boat has sunk by now! We've got to catch the cops attention so they'll know we're inside!" Louis whispered.

Penny listened intently; the sounds were echoing. Someone was approaching in a loud vehicle, an airboat perhaps, maybe several of them. "We could climb out the back window and call to them!" she told Louis quietly.

"It's too dark. The gators might come up onto the deck and we won't be able to see if they do!" Louis pointed out.

Outside, Kerry put on his flashlight hat, stepped up into the driver's seat of his airboat and headed out toward the grassy bog, away from the swamp entrance.

Three well-lighted airboats were coming into view around the bend. Penny squinted, trying to see who was driving. One had two People she didn't recognize. The second contained Max Parker. Jack Sigety sat on the third one with Dante driving.

Alexandra stepped behind Penny in the window and began waving her arms and yelling. "Hey, over here!"

"They aren't turning!" Louis announced, then quickly searched the room and picked up the closest stool. "We've got to break this window and yell!" He told Penny and Alexandra. "We've got to get their attention."

The girls backed up and covered their faces. Louis tossed the stool but it just bounced off the glass. He ran, picked it up and this time he slammed it harder against the dirty pane.

Shattering loudly, the glass finally gave way, catching the attention of all three of the drivers. The airboats turned in unison to head to Airboat Willy's.

"Uncle Max!" Penny yelled at the top of her lungs, waving her hand out of the opening. "Uncle Max!"

The girls were cheering, even Karin had tears in her eyes.

The first off the airboat was Dante. He shut off the engine, leaped onto the deck and tried the door.

Penny heard him tell the officers. "They're locked in."

"Back up!" Max jumped down onto the dock from his airboat seat and crew his handgun. "Move away from the door!"

The girls moved to the corner of the room with Cindy aiding Karin.

"All clear," announced Dante peering into the window, his eyes on his sister and his friend. Then he backed up, too.

Max pulled the trigger. The bullet exploded the lock into several pieces, which flew in all directions.

"We're free!" Penny screamed.

Pushing the door aside, Dante grinned, devilishly, "You two are safe now."

"What happened?" Max questioned Penny.

Instead of answering, Penny jumped into Dante's empty airboat and sat on the driver's bench seat. "We've got to catch Kerry. Come on! Hurry up!"

Chapter 19

"The Marine Patrol is waiting at the entrance of the Swamp. Our first priority is to take you all to safety!" Max announced to Penny. "We'll capture the kidnapper after we're sure you're headed back to the mainland!"

"Kerry could be long gone by then!" Penny turned the key to start the airboat engine. The propeller fan began to twirl. She pressed on the gas pedal and grabbed the rudder stick. "I can't let him go free -not now!"

Max screamed. "You don't even know how to drive that thing. Airboats are very tricky!"

Louis jumped from the dock, landing in Uncle Max's craft just as Penny whirled it around. He stumbled to the driver's seat and pushed her over to the other side of the bench seat. "But I can," he informed.

"Jack, stay here. Kevin, take three of the girls to the Marine Patrol, then make another trip. Don't overload your airboat; it'll sink!" Max demanded.

"Yes, Sir," the man driving the passenger airboat replied.

Penny could barely hear Max barking orders, but she listened long enough to realize the others, numbers one through six, would be well taken care of.

Louis took her hand and put it on top of the rudder stick. "Don't yank too hard. Push it easy, like this."

Surprised he was teaching her, she asked. "You're giving me lessons?"

"You want to learn, don't you?" Louis grinned.

He hadn't smiled for so long, she had almost forgotten how handsome he looked when he did. She returned the gesture. "Do you know where Kerry might go?"

"There are a lot of places we can check out." Louis glanced up. "I'm glad this airboat has high beams."

"Kerry's will be harder to find because he doesn't have them," she remembered.

"If he shuts off his headlight, we're in trouble."

"We've got to hurry then."

Louis tossed the blood-stained shirt that had been tied around his arm into the water. "Don't forget, he's got a gun."

"We'll deal with that once we find him."

Louis looked back. Another airboat with Dante and Uncle Max was following them. "Max will help."

The wind at fifty miles an hour tossled his hair as the boat flew over the saw grass, duckweed and algae-coated water. Louis shouted, "What a rush!"

"See anything?" Penny asked him.

"Nothing. He's got a lead on us."

She glanced back and noticed Uncle Max's larger airboat was having difficulty gaining speed. "Uncle Max won't be able to catch up." Cypress trees looked as if they were flying by.

Suddenly, their craft slammed into a log, raised above the water and slapped back down with a huge splash.

"Be careful," Louis warned. "You can sink an airboat like that, especially in deeper water."

"Tell me what to do."

"Steer around the logs," He showed her how to shift the rudder stick. "This changes the boat's direction."

"Thanks!" She yelled, straining to hear him over the roar of the fan behind them.

The water opened in front of them as surprised gators scurried out of the way and multicolored birds flew off. Penny saw a light to the northeast. "Kerry!"

"Maybe."

"Let's get a better view." She moved the rudder and the boat slid toward the light that was traveling quickly ahead of them.

"Maybe we should slow up for Uncle Max."

"No way!" Moving closer, she could see an airboat. "It is him!"

She hit her foot over Louis' on top of the gas pedal. The boat lurched forward, speeding to over seventy miles an hour.

"Slow down!" Louis ordered. "We'll tip if you keep this up!"

"But We're almost there!" Penny could see Kerry in the driver's seat.

Just then Kerry looked back and his eyes widened in horror as they were closing in on him. He raised the gun and shot at almost the same instant.

Penny took her foot off the gas pedal and the boat skipped over the water, losing momentum.

"Wait for Uncle Max, Penny!"

"But we'll lose him."

Louis returned his foot to the pedal and Penny maneuvered the rudder, continuing to pursue at a slower pace.

Another gunshot sounded.

Louis responded, "Kerry can't get a good shot yet."

As the two airboats jockeyed closer to each other the noise became deafening. Murky water splashed everywhere.

Instantly Kerry's airboat turned 360 degrees to head right for them. If she hadn't seen it herself, she would not have believed the boat's ability to maneuver so quickly.

"What's he doing?" Penny screamed.

Louis grabbed the rudder stick and aided Penny to steer right. The sides of the hulls touched, knocking each other and scrapping up the sides.

Relieved at the near miss, Penny sat back. "Not good enough, Kerry!"

"Turn around!" Louis warned.

At once she saw what Louis was referring to; Kerry hadn't circled because he wanted to attack them. He did so because short poles stuck straight up out of the water, warning signs not to enter the swamp because the water wasn't deep enough. Every few hundred feet a notice was posted. Now she saw them.

Louis took his foot off the pedal while Penny shifted the rudder stick, but it was already too late. The airboat hit a short post and flew three feet into the air. Louis and Penny grabbed the bench seat, holding on for their lives.

"Aaaagh!" Penny screamed.

The stern of the airboat smacked down first. The hull quickly flooded and water began washing over the engine!

Immediately, the motor died. The prop blades started hitting the surface and breaking apart.

Louis yelled. "Jump!"

Penny and Louis together leaped outward and landed on their feet in the shallow water a few feet from the sinking boat. The fan stopped, abruptly, one piece of the propeller dropped out from the cage, but nothing flew out at them.

"We're okay," she realized but could hardly believe it. "Let's wait on the airboat seat for Uncle Max."

Louis nodded in agreement. The two waded back into the water-filled sunken hull and hopped onto the bench seat a few feet above the water and underneath their one remaining light.

Searching behind her, Penny could no longer see Uncle Max's airboat. "They must have gone after Kerry when he flew past us."

"Great," Louis said sarcastically. "We're stuck!"

"They'll come back," she promised, trying to sound upbeat.

Minutes dragged by like hours. Insects hummed and whistled softly in the peaceful surroundings. He raised his foot out of the water and tried to lift one leg over the other. His foot hit Penny's thigh. "You'd think they'd put bigger seats in this thing."

Penny raised her sneakers, remembering the last time she had taken a dip. "Do you think the water's too shallow for gators?"

Louis raised a brow. "They don't even need water."

"I hope Uncle Max catches Kerry soon."

"Even if he doesn't, they'll know who the Numbers Kidnapper is now. They'll be able to capture him sooner or later. At least they've got a name and face attached to the crimes.

"Now that you're a witness, Louie, he'll want you dead, too." Penny reminded him. "How can we play Friday if we have to keep looking over our shoulders for someone with a gun in the stands?"

"You're right," Louis sighed. "I would never have thought Gordan was involved in this either if Kerry hadn't admitted he couldn't wait for Gordan before he killed us."

"Gordan probably did more than we think. Kerry seemed to be more of a watchman."

"Unless we stop them both, we're dead, and they'll be a number nine." A bull frog croaked in seeming agreement.

Penny tried to wring out the bottom of her jeans. Muck water seeped out. "Why take girls by numbers at all?"

"Only Gordan or Kerry can answer that. Do you hear something?" Louis turned his head left and right.

"What?" she wondered, listening. Only faint twitter and an occasional croak echoed around her.

"It sounded like a splash."

Before Penny could agree, a giant gator surfaced. Penny jumped off her side of the seat into the water. Louis did as well. She turned around to see if it was still visible. Nothing.

A few minutes passed before the bumpy-backed reptile appeared again, with open mouth and a long, thin scar right underneath its chin. It snapped at her right side as Penny stumbled back. In a swift move, the enormous beast lurched, pushing her underneath the surface to the sandy bottom.

She wrapped an arm around his snout so the reptile couldn't turn his head and bite her upper body. Long, powerful nails scraped at her legs and arms under the water. Soon her lungs ached for air. Her arms were trembling, trying to lift the enormous gator up. A few more seconds and Penny knew she was going to pass out from the lack of oxygen.

Suddenly, hands reached down and grabbed the gator behind his neck raising it off of her. Penny lifted her head and gasped in air. After her vision cleared from the muddied water, she saw them, Louis wrestling the gator. Struggling, she tried to pull the reptile's leg so he'd release his grip.

"Let him go!" Louis shouted.

"No, Scarface will drone you!"

Another open mouth appeared from behind, a smaller reptile which bit at Scarface's tail. With the weight of both of them, Louis was forced to release the monster. Immediately, the larger gator whipped around and snapped at the intruder.

Together Penny and Louis hurried back into the airboat bench seat to stand and watch the enormous gator being attacked by three smaller reptiles attempting to eat him, one of their injured own.

Penny caught her breath, hardly believing her eyes. "They want him, not us."

"Scarface won't go down without a fight." Louis said. And, he was right. The large beast lashed out at the others. He snapped at one's snout then another. His powerful jaws and size were finally too much for them to conquer. This was more than about food, Penny surmised; it was about who was master of the swamp. After a few more warning bites and much hissing, the smaller reptiles retreated into deeper waters. Scarface quietly lowered into the shallow water and continued to gaze up at Penny and Louis. His big greenish-yellow eyes and rough face were barely visible.

"He's going to try for us again." Louis prepared himself, lowering in the seat to catch him if he jumped.

The gator sunk deeper into the water, resting at the bottom.

Louis tried to reach into the prop to grab a blade. However, the cage rings were too close together. "I can't reach it. No use."

Penny clung to him. "We'll have to fight him off like he did the others."

They wrapped their arms around each other.

Wet and shivering in the dark, they stared at the duckweed. Underneath lurked an ancient foe gathering strength for another attack.

"You two want to join us?" asked a voice.

Penny whirled around. The gator attack prevented her from hearing the airboat approaching. "Uncle Max! Dante!"

Dante smiled. "You guys go for a swim?" He threw her a line to pull their craft next to their half-sunken one.

"Watch out, there's a huge gator down there!" Penny pointed.

Max's hand moved to his gun. "I've got you covered."

Penny and Louis pulled in the line. Penny stepped out first; Louis followed, keeping his eyes on the water below. Safely onboard, they crossed to the passenger seat in the front and sat down underneath the two driver's seats.

"Did you catch Kerry?" Penny asked Max.

"He got away," Dante answered for him. "His boat's a racer."

"Which way did he go?" Louis questioned.

Max pointed north.

"Maybe he went to the Front Street dock," Louis reminded Dante of the place.

"Yeah," Dante started the propeller. "Airboat Willy's used to pick up half of their dining customers up there because of the parking lot where people could leave their cars."

Their boat turned and rumbled toward the bright northern star over the algae- covered water. Now resting, Penny surveyed her gator scratches, then glanced back to their abandoned airboat. What she saw made her skin crawl. There, climbing up onto the driver's seat where Louis and she had just been was Scarface, King of the Swamp.

Chapter 20

Max reached underneath the driver's seat and pulled out his Police pacset radio. "This is Alpha 9 requesting 1057 in the vicinity of US1 and the Front Street loading dock."

Penny couldn't make out the dispatcher's response over the roar of the propeller. Max must have had listening problems too, she realized, because he covered his opposite ear to hear better.

The airboat slid into a small canal. Spanish moss hung like a canopy over the water, tangling around the high beam light on the top of the boat. Louis wiped some off. "Are the other girls okay?"

Max repeated the question into the receiver, then loudly announced. "Five of them are on their way to the Indialantic Police Station. Karin's going to the hospital."

"How's her leg?" Penny asked.

"They think it's a clean break."

Penny raised her arms in praise. "Yes! She'll be doing back flips in no time!"

Max shut off the motor and the airboat slid quietly out of the swamp channel into the salty Indian river.

By the shoreline, Kerry McLoy was busily loading his airboat onto the white minivan's trailer. He wasn't even hurrying thought Penny.

The moment he saw them coming out into the open, he yanked out his gun.

Max jumped from his seat and raised his. "Drop your weapon now!"

Kerry shouted. "I'll shoot you dead! I will!"

Max pushed Penny's head. "Everybody down."

Penny, Louis and Dante knelt, then flattened out in the hull of the boat as the criminal and the cop stared at one another. She could hear police sirens coming from both directions on the dirt road leading to the loading dock.

"It's your choice, Kerry. You can lower your gun or go out with a bang when the Melbourne PD arrive," Max said.

He's trying to avoid bloodshed Penny decided. Peering over the side she saw three police cars barreling down the dirt road with clouds of dirt following their back wheels. Within a matter of moments three blue and whites surrounded the van, screeching to a stop. Their car doors burst open and six officers jumped out with their guns raised.

"I've got him!" Max yelled. "Everybody take it easy!"

Again, Penny peeked over the edge of the hull. Kerry's eyes moved to hers. His gun swung around, aiming toward her head.

Immediately, Max pulled his trigger. Bang!

Kerry's gun flew out of his hand. Instantly, Max leaped out of the boat, over the ramp, and tackled Kerry to the ground.

Four officers rushed to apprehend him.

Penny sat up, her body shaking while she watched Kerry's hands being cuffed behind his back. "They got him."

Louis and Dante slipped out of the boat and pulled the airboat to the sandy shore. Penny waited. She gazed at Kerry being read his rights then led to the back of a police car. He kept looking at her, reminding her of the cold, reptilian stare of Scarface.

"You need help?" Louis asked, his hand extended to her.

"I'll be all right." Penny stepped out of the boat onto the pavement, trying to control her trembling even now.

"I need you three to come to the station and give statements." Max brushed a duckweed off his shoulder.

"First, we have to hurry home to the Bulldog party, Dante said, "before Mom and Dad realize we're missing."

"They'll be plenty of time for parties after you three win the Championship."

"No, you don't understand." Penny gripped his tight arm. "Kerry's brother was involved in this. I don't know how much, but Gordan McLoy will be at this party!"

Max interrogated, "Why do you think this Gordan fellow had anything to do with the Numbers Kidnapper?"

"Kerry told us."

Louis confirmed. "She's right; we've got to capture Gordan or we're all still in danger."

"Did any of you actually see him at the swamp near the victims or hear of the girls speak of another attacker?"

"One said she heard someone," Penny recalled.

"So no one actually saw Gordan or can tie him directly to the crimes?" Max questioned.

"Just Kerry," Penny replied.

"Then we've got work to do."

"Can I help?" Penny inquired.

"Yes, you all can." Max led the three of them to a police car and took the keys from one of the officers. "I'll bring it back to the Melbourne station after I'm done," he announced.

The officer asked. "Need any assistance?"

"Give us a few minutes, then contact Jack Sigety at the Indialantic Station."

"What's the 1020?" He asked.

"Tell him to meet me at the Margarita's on South Patrick Road. He'll know where it is."

"Sure, Max."

"Now, you two," Max turned to Louis and Penny. "On our way to your house we'll discuss how to handle this situation."

"Gordan probably won't put up much of a fight since he doesn't know we're onto him," Penny said.

"No, my Dear," Max checked his shiny silver watch. "I'm speaking of your Father. He's going to be a real Bugger since we're late to his shindig."

Chapter 21

Max opened the front door to the Margarita house. Penny, Louis and Dante walked in. The fights flew on.

"Go Bulldogs, go!"

The cheers faded as expressions turned from celebration to worry.

Penny examined herself. She realized that she was wet from head to toe. Her arms were covered with green algae and bloodied scratches from Scarface. She glanced at Louis. Topless with duckweed sticking out of his hair, Louis didn't look any better.

"We're okay," Penny claimed. "We went for a swim in the river."

Instantly, they were bombarded by hug after hug, Penny got embraced from family members and teammates. Her grandmother called her, "Petykoya," then pinched her cheeks. Tyrom slapped her on the butt. The Coach gave her a high-five. Her mother kissed her on the forehead.

"Where did you two swim," her mother questioned, "a sewage dump?"

"We'll explain later, Mom."

"Max, did you have anything to do with this?" Dr. Margarita frowned. "Weren't you supposed to be keeping a close eye on them?"

"We're fine, Dad. Dante even went with us."

Her father glanced to Dante. "At least one of my kids was smart enough to stay out of the water."

Dante chuckled. "I'd never swim in…"

"Enough, Son." Dr. Margarita interrupted. "You three should have been here more than a half hour ago."

Penny put his hand on his father's shoulder. "Come on, Pops, it's our party. Let's have fun."

"We'll discuss this later." Dr. Margarita grabbed a glass and walked to the center of the room.

Max stated. "I'll have to let him win at golf next weekend."

The party began with Dr. Margarita making a speech. "Thank you all for coming in honor of Penny's quick recovery. I want you all to know that my wife and I have never been so proud of our daughter as we are today. Not only did she handle this kidnapping crisis courageously, she is going to help bring the State Championship to Indialantic High. Three cheers for Penny and the Bulldogs. Hip-Hip Hurrah!"

The crowd joined in while Penny tried to hide the crimson coming to her cheeks. "Hip-Hip Hurrah! Hip-Hip Hurrah!"

Dr. Margarita held up his sparkling crystal glass filled with white wine. "Adults, the bar's open. For you young'uns there is food and dancing. So let's enjoy this glorious evening, shall we!"

The crowd started dispersing into groups, some heading for the open bar, others rushing towards the tour food tables. A few couples started gyrating to the DJ music. The Coach went to admire the giant cake shaped like the Bulldog's pawprint emblem.

It took Penny a few minutes but she found Gordan in a corner of the living room, sitting next to Frank on the sofa. She strolled immediately to Louis and Max Parker. "What's the plan?"

Louis told her. "Uncle Max wants us to find out what Gordan knows. You stay here and handle the party."

Hey, Gordan," Louis called to him on the sofa. "Dante and I want to show you something." Louis waved for him to come.

Gordan handed Frank his cup of punch and followed Louis and Dante up the stairs. Penny couldn't stand it; something was about to go down and they were leaving her out of it. She bolted after them.

Max grabbed her before she could enter Dante's bedroom. "Penny, they'll do this."

"Not without me they won't." She ripped her good arm out of his grasp and flew into the room.

Max stepped back into the shadows.

"What is it, Louie?" Gordan questioned, leaning against the large bay window.

"We discovered who the Numbers Kidnapper is?"

"Really?" Gordan sounded intrigued. "Who might that be?"

"Kerry, your brother." Louis announced.

Penny positioned herself between Dante and Louis. "And, you!"

Gordan crossed his arms. "You're kidding, right?"

"You knew Kerry was kidnapping all those girls, didn't you?" Penny swallowed down her anger.

"What? Are you crazy?"

"Kerry couldn't have taken those girls on his own. You helped him."

"No!"

"What sick things were you planning to do to them and me that the police should know about?"

"You wouldn't go to the cops and tell them this nonsense?"

"Yes, I most certainly will."

Gordan yanked out a gun from behind his back, his expression turning dark and sinister. "You can't!" Gordan quickly cocked his weapon and placed a silencer over the barrel. "Not until our sister, number 9, disappears."

Dante held his hands out, stepping in front of Penny. "Why your own sister? Why mine?"

"They're all the same, Dante. The girls all want to steal our glory. Don't you see? Your sister is just like Shara. She couldn't stand that Kerry received more press for his hockey scores than she got for her stupid volleyball tournaments. She and Kerry fought and my brother fell out of the second story window. Now Kerry, a real athlete, is crippled for life."

Penny shouted out. "My Dad would have helped Kerry find a good doctor! Maybe his hip could be fixed with surgery!"

The gun shook in his hands. Sweat began beading off his chin. "There's no hope for him. Just like you took my dreams away from me."

Dante kicked hard, knocking the gun from Gordan's hands. Louis jumped and grabbed him, wrapping his arms behind his back. Dnate raised his fist to hit Gordan in the mouth.

"Wait!" Penny cried out. "He'll have his day in court."

"We've got alibis. During three of the kidnappings, I was at tryouts. I'll say Kerry was watching me from the stands" Gordan didn't seem too concerned. "It'll wind up your word against mine. No pig will arrest us. They'll take one look at Kerry's bad leg, my schedule, and let us go."

"Wrong," Max popped into the room holding out his gun with one hand, a tiny tape recorded in the other. "Taped your whole confession."

"There you are, Uncle." Penny smiled.

"Had him covered the whole time." He lifted the gun with a pen then started pulling out a pair of handcuffs. "We'll just see what happens to you. Got word just a little while ago that the little leaguer came out of her coma. It seems she's having a heyday describing her two attackers to the police."

Gordan's face went pale. "No! She's dead! The doctors said she's dying!"

Jack Sigety came in. "No such luck. My associates as we speak are getting a confession from your brother, Kerry. He's saying the kidnappings were all your idea."

"Now who's the loser?" Penny stood in front of Gordan, her eyes filled with rage.

"Shut up, Witch. The jury will understand. You girls should have stayed in your place!"

Her hands tightened into fists. "Where's that?"

"The sidelines."

Her fist flew back and punched him dead in the nose. Max shoved her back gently. "I'll take it from here."

The three of them watched Gordan being read his rights by Jack Sigety, then escorted out of the bedroom. The party below stopped, abruptly. Everyone stared at Gordan coming down the stairs in handcuffs.

"Either one of you feel like cutting a rug?" Penny questioned her brother and the young man who had captured her heart.

Dante and Louis broke away to the middle of the living room. Their hands flew out for her to join them.

Penny hurried to them. "Oh, I see what you boys want," Penny began shaking her hips to the song the DJ was playing, Jimmy Buffet's "Margaritavilla."

"It's about time we get this party started!"

Chapter 22

The next morning...

Penny wrote a note and folded it into thirds on top of her desk. A shadow crossed the wall in front of her. She turned her head to see her brother sitting on her bed.

"What are you doing?" Dante questioned.

She swiveled her desk chair to face him. "Writing Louis' Dad a note."

He lay down, putting his hands behind his head. "Don't bother."

Penny read the letter.

Dear Mr. Windsor,

I'm leaving you a ticket. Louis wants you to come, although I doubt he's going to ask you. For the past four years you've never attended a game; that's why he's stopped trying. I can't understand why you wouldn't support him when he loves you so much. Louis is a really wonderful person and I know you must see that in him too, I hope you do, Sir, because you're the one who raised him to be this way. Louis is a loyal and great friend, he has been there for me through the scariest time in my life. I think he's been there for you, too, taking you to your AA meetings. Now, he needs you more than ever. Don't let him down. Please attend the Championship. I'm asking you, Sir, to take an active role in celebrating what a brilliant man your son has become. You see, it doesn't matter if the Bulldogs win or lose. All that does is that we have the people we love there the most to pat us on the back either way.

Kind regards,
Margarita #8.

Dante shook his head. "Nice try, but he still won't come."

"It's worth a shot." Penny took out an envelope from her top desk drawer.

"You really think a lot of Louie, don't you?"

Penny put the ticket and note inside the white container. "Yes."

"Are you two dating or girlfriend and boyfriend yet?"

"I don't know. We've been so busy with the games and the Numbers Kidnappers; it's hard to say exactly what we are."

"Do you want to be his girlfriend?"

Penny nodded.

"Louis is a lucky man." Dante gazed at her with his dark blue gems. "You'd be faithful not like those tramps I always wind up with."

"Maybe you should pick with your brains and not other parts of your body." Penny commented. "Chose a girl you can be friends with first."

"What's the point. I can't seem to find good friends either. I never would have thought Gordan capable of kidnapping girls. I can hardly believe it."

"I know, his guilt gives me the creeps. Think of all the times he's been at our house for parties."

"At least with the girlfriends I pick, I get laid."

"Stop it." Penny swallowed, turning crimson. "Besides, your friends aren't all bad. What about Louis and Frank?"

"Oh, Frank's a real gem. He likes you too?"

"What?" Penny gasped. "No he doesn't."

"Why else would he have gone to the hospital and apologized?"

Penny angrily raised her tone. "Because he thinks I'm a talented quarterback!"

Dante acknowledged. "Maybe."

"He admitted he was wrong, Dante, That's more than you ever would."

"True, but he never had to live with you."

Penny straightened. The rage in her heart dissipating. "A friend of mine told me she thinks you act like a jerk to me because you're tired of living in David's shadow. Is that true?"

"What are you talking about?"

"Are you jealous of how much I loved David?"

"You're nuts."

"Does my being a QB only remind you that David and I were closer than you and me?"

Dante stared up at the ceiling. "David liked you better."

"He treated us equally. He asked you to play with him and help him warm up too, remember?"

Tears welled in his eyes. "Yeah, but I never said yes."

She turned around and wrote, "Mr. Windsor," on the envelope. She didn't know what to say to Dante. Hugging him was the only thing that came to mind but she felt weird running over to the bed and embracing her brother when she had deemed him as the biggest jerk for the past year.

Suddenly, she felt arms wrap around her from behind. She saw Dante leaning over her in the mirror.

"I've been taking my missing him out on you, haven't I?"

She placed her hand on his arm and rubbed, gently. "It's all right."

He grinned. "I would say I love you and I'm glad you re okay but I think you'd barf."

She snickered. "I'd try not to."

"I love you, then."

Penny faked vomiting. "I love you, too.

Chapter 23

Mobbed by fans and reporters, the bus came to a stop outside the Tampa Bay Stadium. The Bulldogs, one by one, began to exit. As they moved past, Penny noticed that they were all wearing their new matching Bulldogs caps and jackets. Quickly, she reached into her gym bag, pulled out the shiny, bright blue clothing and put hers on.

She followed the team inside the terminal. She held her head high, not wanting to appear nervous while the cameras snapped their shots.

"Penny, the Saint's manager told me you're changing room is number 23, last room down this hall," the Coach said above the noise of the media.

She rushed away to where he had told her, a men's bathroom. She almost laughed. Maybe this was a way that the St. Petersburg Saints were trying to get to her.

She closed her eyes trying to get her emotions in check before she put on her uniform. Only a few more minutes until the game begins. She has to pull herself together now, for her team. She's made it to this point, climbed that mountain with an almost flawless season. It was her blood, her tears, that helped get the Bulldogs to this point. She can't back down or be scared, not for one second. This is the game she's waited for all her life.

Quickly, she dressed. Then, she took one last look at herself in the mirror wearing her #8 jersey. It felt good, felt right.

There was a knock on the bathroom door. "You decent, Penny?"

She recognized the voice. "Come in, Frank."

He sauntered into the bathroom in full uniform and gear, "Nice place you got here." He glared at the stalls.

"A real palace," Penny said sarcastically. "So what's up? We've got a game to win."

"I wanted to thank you for talking to the Coach and having me put back on the team. He said he'd only play me a few minutes, but it's still better than nothing."

"No problem."

"I guess since you spoke on my behalf, you know that I wouldn't have been friends with Gordan if I knew he was planning to hurt you or anybody else."

"Gordan and Kerry kidnapped all the numbers by themselves, Kerry confessed."

"Good, then you believe me."

"Have you seen Louis' Dad in a seat by my parents? I left him an envelope inside his mailbox with a ticket."

"Near Al5, no. Mr. Windsor never comes to the Bulldog games, Penny."

"I know. I just hoped that maybe he'd show up for the Championship. Don't tell Louis that I left him one."

Frank inched closer. "No problem. There's another reason I came to see you, Penny. I wanted to give you something."

"What?" Penny began checking her shoulder pads.

"I knew your brother, David. He was a group counselor at the Wilson Football Camp for Kids."

Frank held out a tiny black box to her. "At the time, I wasn't built like I am today. The other camp kids used to pick on me. David volunteered to work with me that summer in the gym to get me ready for Hawk Jr. High School's tryouts."

"You never told me that."

"I don't like to think about those days much." He gave her the box. "The morning before David died he came to my school for the Hawk tryouts. He stayed awhile, gave me advice, and a couple of things. He said that they always brought him luck. That year I made a football team for the first time."

She flipped the lid open. A small necklace fell into her fingers. It was silver with a small football charm carved near the laces, the number 8. She pictured David in her mind's eye, his big smile with the necklace shimmering underneath. "This was David's. I remember!"

"He also gave me a bandanna. I've given that to Dante."

"You're letting me keep it?"

"I figured David would want you to have his chain along with his number." Frank reopened the door.

"Wait." Penny wiped her tearing eyes. "Thanks Frank."

"Don't thank me. You deserve it. You're amazing. Now, let's go out there and win the championship!"

Penny stuffed on her Bulldog's helmet and stormed through the doorway toward the tunnel where the rest of the players were lining up. She heard Frank yelling, "Let's do it for David!" while they walked. Pride raced through her veins.

Names and numbers were being called over the loudspeakers, signaling the Bulldog team members to run onto the field. She heard every inhale and exhale. Everything seemed to be going in slow motion. The cool night air seemed to be making smoke come out of her mouth. Her feet seemed to float on the grass as "Margarita #8" was called.

Underneath the bright Tampa stadium lights she had never seen so many people in all her life. She jogged to her mark, slapping the hands of the Bulldog line all the way. The crowd roared.

In the spotlight, Miss USA started singing "The Star Spangled Banner." Penny removed her helmet. A smile crossed her lips as the high note of the song made her proud to be where she was. Where else in the world, could a woman play a game like this?

Jacob and Dante went to the center of the field for the coin toss.

"Heads!" Jacob yelled.

"Bulldogs win the toss!" claimed the announcer.

"We defer!" Jacob informed.

Referee nodded and yelled, "Saints ball!"

The game started with the Saints grinding out a seven-minute drive on their first possession. When the Saints finally made it into the red zone, they choked. The Bulldogs held them to a field goal. They then kicked off and the Bulldogs Special Teams took the ball all the way to the fifty-yard line. Penny quickly made three completions to Louis for a touchdown.

End of the First Quarter: Bulldogs 7 Saints 3

For the second quarter the Saints began to excel. Two drives, two touchdowns. The Bulldogs couldn't accomplish much with two offensive lineman down with injuries.

End of the Second Quarter: Bulldogs 7 Saints 17

Penny was sacked at the beginning of the third. She was slow to get up but managed to toss a forty-yard touchdown pass to Tyrom. Then, with the Saints still leading by a field goal, they took control of the ball. The Saints drove the Bulldog defense all the way to the thirty-yard line and were able to run the touchdown in due to a missed tackle by Dante.

End of the Third Quarter: Bulldogs 14 Saints 24

By the start of the fourth quarter, Penny was favoring one leg. The Saint defenders played on this new weakness and at every opportunity hit her leg. She was dragging because of the injury, making it very easy for them to get sacks. She got knocked off her feet four times in the drive.

Somehow, she managed to throw a quick pass to Jacob and he ran it down to the thirty yard line where they were able to make a field goal.

For several minutes the Saints maintained possession. Their running back was held up by Frank in the red zone. On fourth down, the kick dropped wide left of the goal posts, no good.

Bulldogs returned to the field with five minutes to go. They ran the ball to protect Penny as much as possible. Saints wouldn't let them gain more than three yards a carry. Finally, during the fourth attempt the Saints misread the play and Louis caught a screen pass for the first down on the Saints forty-yard line.

Next play, Penny was sacked. Saints got a late hit penalty charge for fifteen yards. She got up, yanked the grass out of her helmet and threw a twenty-five-yard touchdown to Tyrom.

Saints had two minutes.

Tie ball game.

Saints failed, one , two, three and out. Punted for sixty yards.

Penny glanced over to the Coach who signaled a down and out play to Tyrom with only a minute left on the clock. The play went miserably and she took another quarterback sack before she could get the ball off.

The second attempt was a left pass pattern which was caught by the tight end. He took it to the fifty yard line, first down.

Coach tried a running play next to throw the defense off balance. Jacob wobbled the ball, gained possession, then quickly jumped out of bounds with only six seconds left.

Penny called time.

She could barely feel anything but the pain throbbing down her leg.

"Is it your knee?" Louis asked in the huddle.

"Yeah."

"How bad?" Jacob sounded worried.

"I'll live. One more touchdown to throw."

The circle of players looked at each other. Only six seconds remained until they went into overtime. They seemed all to be beaten, exhausted mental and physically. Penny searched their eyes and saw a willingness to give up on these last seconds for a better chance in overtime. "We can do this." Through the jersey, she clung to her charm. "We can't risk the Saints winning the toss! We have to go for it now!"

Louis took a deep breath. "They're all over me like a bad suit. It's hard to catch when I'm being triple covered."

Penny glanced over to where her parents were sitting in the first row, center field. There they were. Her mom and Dad, clapping and cheering for the Bulldogs. A familiar face was sitting behind them. "Louis, your Dad's here. Pull something out of your Houdini hat for him."

Louis stuck his head up, searching the seats.

"He's right by my parents."

Louis's face widened with glee. "My Dad actually showed up!"

"A lot can happen in six seconds. Are you going to let your Dad think you're a quitter the first time he's ever seen you play!"

"No way!" Louis promised. "Come on, guys. Penny's right and we know it! This is the Championship! We can't risk giving up the ball."

"Let's see if the Saints have a holy defense! Let's go. Rock-n-Baby." Penny clapped out of the huddle. Rock-n-Baby meant that Louis would break right while the rest of the offensive play was designed to go left. Penny went to maintain her position. She looked one more time in the stands. She thought she saw someone sitting next to Louis' Dad. She dismissed it; immediately, the play clock was winding down.

She called, "hut 29, hut 29, hut hut." She pushed back in pain and her knee gave way. As she was tumbling back, she mustered all her might and let one go as hard as she could.

A lineman was on top of her as she watched that ball go straight to heaven. She prayed God, then, to give it wings to fly straight where she had intended.

She felt the crunch of her bones as another massive Saint toppled over her. Her eyes closed tightly.

Then, she heard it over the roar of the crowd. "Touchdown! Touchdown Louis Windsor! Bulldogs win!"

The buzzer sounded.

Two Saints jumped off of her in shock. Penny lifted at the waist to see Louis holding the ball in the corner of the end zone. He was jumping up and down as the fans began storming onto the field.

"Bulldogs won by a touchdown!" repeated the commentator.

Penny got up favoring her right leg. Players were rushing toward her bruised body. They slapped her helmet while the reporters scurried to the scene. Overwhelmed with emotions, she cried tears of joy. Her parents were alternating between jumping and hugging. Dante leaped into the first row to embrace them.

The figure in the seat next to Louis' father was applauding enthusiastically; the ghostly image wore jersey #8.

Penny called to him from the field. "Thanks for coming, Partner!"

Dozens of microphones were suddenly stuck in her face. "Penny, how do you feel being the first female ever to win the State Football Championship?" she heard over the shouts from the sea of blue and black jerseys.

The Coach, drenched with Gatorade, handed her the trophy for their victory pictures. "This one is for my brother!" She announced. She peered over reporters' heads at the shimmering figure. "He died before he could get ever get to play in a Championship game! I dedicate this trophy to David Margarita." Her voice shook with emotion.

Louis suddenly came from behind and raised her onto his shoulders. The people began chanting, "Pen-ny! Pen-ny! Pen-ny!"

David's reflection began disappearing in the midst of the colorful fireworks. Confetti and blue paper streamers flew all about as she held out the golden trophy toward him, then raised it high above her head. He blew her a kiss in response. Ecstatically she screamed, "We did it! We did it!"

Chapter 24

Penny and Louis sat on the bench overlooking Flutie Athletic Park. A few mothers were there, pushing their toddlers on the swings or helping them climb into the large wooden maze.

They watched the little kids play for awhile, then decided to check out the baseball diamond. Holding hands they moved across the empty soccer field to lounge on the bleachers and search for one particular child.

With short blonde hair and bright green eyes, Penny pondered if the girl at bat could be her. "She looks just like a miniature Sarah McLoy." She commented. "Her haircut and thin nose; maybe, she's number 61, Debra Jamison?"

"Are you sure you're up to meeting anyone? How's the knee?"

"I'm fine. I've made a decision." Penny informed. "I want to go to Western Florida University with you."

"Your chances of playing your first year are better with the Sea Eagles."

"The Eagles don't have Coach Johnson: Western Florida does. I could learn a lot from him. In the long run that's best for my football career. Besides, there's one thing that means more to me than being a quarterback." She gazed into his hazel pools. "You."

"Would you like to be my girlfriend then?"

"What?"

"I think we should take this dating thing to the next level." He pulled her close and kissed her lips. "So how about it?"

"Yes, I'd would love to be."

"Then it's settled. We're officially boyfriend and girlfriend."

"This calls for celebration!" Penny feathered her fingers through his curly locks.

"Deli's Ice Cream?"

"Double scoops of rocky road."

Louis laid his championship ring on top of hers, clasping her fingers. "All right!"

Debra, recognizing them, ran for the bleachers. "It's you! It's really you two!" Her eyes lit up as if she was witnessing some super hero in a comic strip. "Margarita and Windsor!"

"Are you Debra Jamison?" Penny noticed the circles underneath her big, green eyes.

"Yupper doodles. How'd you guess?"

"You remind me of someone."

"Sarah Mcloy, I heard about her from the others. They said we're like twins."

"You certainly appear a lot alike."

"So is the leg letter? I saw you hurt your knee on TV."

"The sprain is healing. How's your head?"

"Fine." She twirled a curl of her hair. "Did you know you're the first female football Champion in the state of Florida!"

"And you look great at second base." Penny praised "You're still playing, right?"

"South Beach Little League is over with now. But I'm going to sign up again next year. My arm's good as new. I can still hit 'em to the fence." She fidgeted off the seat. "You want me to show you. My mom needs to take a break."

The woman who had been tossing the balls to Debra had moved to the picnic table by the bathrooms, drinking thirstily from a soda can.

"I wish I could, but my leg's all bandaged up."

Louis spoke up. "I'll pitch to you, Debra. Maybe Penny could just stand by the fence and throw the balls back to me, the one you miss."

She tugged on Louis' sleeve for him to follow. "Okay, but I don't let many get by!"

With her mother's permission the three of them headed into the baseball diamond. Debra began swinging the bat, warming up her arms. Penny put on the glove. Louis moved to the pitcher's mound.

"Throw me a fast ball," Debra yelled to Louis.

"I got thunder for fingers, lightning for a hand!"

"Sure, you do." Debra giggled. "Don't go easy on me."

Louis wound up the ball, exaggerating. He spit on the mound and delivered one so fast Penny couldn't see the ball coming. Debra leaned to it and swung. Wham! The ball flew upward and caromed off the back field fence.

"Wow!" Penny exclaimed, not expecting someone so young to hit that far. "You've got a great swing, Debra."

"No kidding!" Louis' mouth hung open.

"I'm going to play for the Chicago Cubs someday. I want to hit a homer right out of Wrigley field."

"You go, Girl!" Penny believed she could. "I can hear Chip Caray announcing you now."

"It might happen as long as the numbers kidnapper doesn't come after me again."

Louis readied himself for another pitch. He waited until Debra was set, then dropped back and uncorked a wild toss that sailed off the plate. Debra didn't swing.

"Nice try," She yelled back at him.

Penny retrieved the ball and quickly hobbled to home plate. "Gordan and Kerry are being tried as adults, Debra. They'll be in jail for a long time. Don't even think about them anymore." She flung it back to Louis then returned to the fence.

He rifled another, changing the ball's speed, trying to keep Debra off balance.

Debra swung. The ball hit the corner of the bat and popped up and into the soccer field, "Foul ball!" She waited for Louis to trot after it, then turned and faced Penny. "I heard more than two voices when I was tied up in the back of the van."

Penny felt her heart skip a beat. "Did you tell the FBI that?"

"The other six told them that they only saw Gordan and Kerry." Debra informed simply, "No one believes me."

Penny wondered if she was joking. "Well, it's not funny to tell people things that aren't true."

"I may have been blindfolded then, but in my dreams I know I hear at least three voices."

Penny relaxed. She, too, was having terrible nights, picturing everything from needles coming to life to Scarface jumping out of her closet. Post-traumatic Stress, her father told her.

"So you've been having nightmares?"

She nodded yes.

"My dad is a doctor. He told me they'll go away after awhile."

Debra checked her swing. The curve ball bounced to the fence.

Louis screamed, "Strike! I got you! I got you!"

Debra argued. "It was left of the plate, ball 2."

Louis ran up to her, pretending to be steaming mad. "It was a Strike."

"Ball!"

"Strike!"

"Ball!" She kicked the dirt. "You got nothing on me!"

Penny interrupted, acting like an empire. "That's enough, you two, break it up!"

"Just try that on me again, Pitcher!"

"I will!" Louis whirled around, turning flamboyantly on one heel.

While he hurried back to the mound, Debra swung the bat over her shoulder and looked Penny in the eye. "So does it get any easier?"

Penny shrugged. "Does what get any easier?"

"Being accepted."

Penny understood. "I think respect eventually comes with talent. Maybe by the time you're my age there won't be as many problems with coed teams."

Debra tapped her baseball cap. "It doesn't matter to me who likes me or not, so long as I can play."

Penny watched Debra hit a slider down the first base line.

Louis ran to the girl and hugged her. "That was a very difficult pitch, my best one!"

Debra laughed, "Told you, you've got nothing on me."

Louis started tickling her underneath her chin. Penny observed how sweet he was to her. What an amazing man! Louis would make a fine husband someday, even a considerate father, she surmised. How lucky she is to have him in her life, to have parents who love her and be talented at a game most women wouldn't even want to play.

"You remind me of my girlfriend." Louis pointed to Penny.

"I do?" Debra smiled. "Why is that?"

The sun sparkling above cast their shadows across the diamond. Penny limped over and wrapped her arms around them both. Their shadows; one.

Louis explained. "You're like magic."

"Magic?"

"You're on that magic carpet, riding all the way to the top!"